A WELL EXECUTED
PIECE OF WORK

"A singular book. The rueful, observant, engaging narrator is found working construction on a high-priced resort island, employed about an eccentric subdivision owned by a family of islanders who would seem to be bred out of Dostoyevsky by—whom?—maybe Eugene O'Neil, maybe Aeschylus. Mr. Mascia has written a psychological novel, original and intense, that its readers will not soon forget."
        —Castle Freeman Jr., author of *The Devil in the Valley*

"Joseph M. Mascia is the best writer about real work since Steinbeck."
        —Howard Frank Mosher, winner of the New England Book Award for Fiction for *A Stranger in the Kingdom*

"Joseph M. Mascia is a mesmerizing and immensely compelling writer."
        —Sara J. Henry, award winning author of *A Cold and Lonely Place*

A Well Executed Piece of Work

by

Joseph M. Mascia

Gavilan Books™

Gavilan Books™ LLC
Vermont, United States of America

Cover Design and Book Design by Gloria J. Cristelli

Photos Used in Cover Design by Joseph M. Mascia

Gavilan Books Logo Design by John J. Mascia

Photo of Joseph M. Mascia on the Back Cover by Juan De Leon

ISBN: 978-0-9989172-0-7

In memory of
Aurora, Helen, Madeline, and Marcia

"As for the residue of the Pequod's company, be it said, that at the present day not one in two of the many thousand men before the mast employed in the American whale fishery, are American born, though pretty nearly all the officers are."

—Herman Melville, *Moby Dick*, Chapter 27

"When years ago we found the whaling business rapidly going down ... We built a great cotton mill ... And we share-holders were eager and anxious that everybody's sons and daughters, SAVE OUR OWN, should leave their pianos, their embroidery, their legal, medical and theological studies and pull off their fashionable coats and roll up their fashionable sleeves and go to work from Monday morning until Saturday night, sixteen hours daily in our cotton mill."

—Prentice Mulford, quoted in Everett T. Rattray's, *The South Fork* (emphasis in the original)

"There was a ghost story about a riveter having been sealed up alive between her [the *Great Eastern*'s] hulls and a general belief that his ghost had put a jinx on the ship. The story was not a sailors' superstition, for a workman's skeleton actually was found inside the ship's shell when the great white elephant was finally broken up in 1889."

—Jeanette Edwards Rattray, from *Ship Ashore!*

Table of Contents

Chapter One

"In the End All Things Will Be Known."

1.

OW THEY SLEEP. The sleep of the just. While I scribble. And pace. And wander the grounds. Haunting the place. Haunted. Somebody used that word not long ago to describe my appearance. I stared at him. Not for too long, I hope. "How'd you guess?" I wanted to say. Or is it that obvious? She studies my face as well, in a proprietary way. Concerned. There's no deluding her. She avoids certain questions; avoids certain topics. There's no deceiving her. My token efforts are simply attempts at deflection; distraction. "It's nothin darlin. Jest workin on my poultry, ha-ha." My poultry. Night after night. I'll have to come up with some sonnets. Something to show. Bad sonnets that I can staple to the end of this before it gets— what? Before it finds its final resting place. Before it finds its home. Distract her with the notion of my own delusion. She's not buying it. Wouldn't matter how many bad sonnets I tacked on. "Cultivatin my delusions, darlin. Where would we be without our delusions?" She knows better. I know she knows better. She knows that I know that she knows better. I know that she knows—Sleep, dear one. Try to sleep. I'll bear this weight. This burden is all mine.

I picture him out there—alive. Not here, haunting the place. Crawling around under the cottages. On one of his nocturnal missions. Instead out there, very much alive; very much out of his mind, having endured just too much that was completely unacceptable. Out there in the woods in a loin cloth, sticks and leaves in his beard, mud and clay smeared artistically and strategically. Roasting cats. Assembling his legal team: a flock of turkeys. Planning his next moves. Planning his comeback. Lording it over a pack of squirrels who he has under his thumb. Who owe everything to him. He still cracks me up, see? He doesn't haunt me. I picture him alive. I can do that, and it doesn't even qualify as a first class self-delusion. A Cat V self-delusion. I never saw it happen. Never saw him down there. Didn't even have to help cover it all up. I had good help. You can't get good help these days? I had good help. Good help acting in self-defense. Ladies and gentlemen of the jury— Won't fly, I'm afraid. Won't do. Completely unacceptable.

Who, having at least a glimmer of self-knowledge isn't a little horrified in studying his own reflection? Like that poor slob in Michelangelo's Last Judgment. There's a man who gets it. And for the rest, what are their lives if not a progression, a regular parade of dreams and self-delusions? They'll get over them eventually, though many won't lose their last delusion until they draw their last breath. He was less delusional than many, was Junior, and not the worst person in the world. Not even close. Not even the worst I've ever met. He could be phenomenally amusing in the way that people who don't have the usual filters between their brains and their mouths are amusing. Said the things that everybody else thinks without saying? He said the things nobody else even thinks. Extremely bright. And extremely funny. If it sounds like I miss him, I readily confess it. Confession #1. If that seems grotesquely ironic, what can I say? That's life. All over. If this narrative turns out a rambling, incoherent mess, so be it. I'll do this one last thing the way I want to. If it kills me. Now, though I have plenty more on my mind and nothing else to do before morning, and not a chance, not the ghost of a chance of a little sleep, I'll intentionally set this aside and stare at the fire in the stove in front of me. Indolence and sloth as an expression of free will. Must be what they were all doing all those years, by the way. My help. My so-called help. In retrospect so much of this sad tale seems to follow inevitably, almost to have been preordained, as though to make a mockery of free will. And how else to express free will except by doing that which appears counterintuitive, by doing that which appears to make no sense? And here I am continuing to write instead of staring stupidly at the fire.

Increasingly easy to do that, it seems. Fires, by the way, and fireplaces figure not a little in the matter at hand, the matter under consideration. The case before the court. Not the catastrophic variety. The climax to this tale is more mundane. More down to earth. Earthy. It's just that I build them. Fireplaces. Or used to. Hearths. You know, hearth and home? *What the fambly used to set around of an evenin after supper? Maw with her mendin and Paw with the Good Book open, and little Jess and Tommy droppin off to dreamland?* That kind. Before that all became obsolete. What with big screen TV in every room and the Internet and Game Boy and *sechlike*. And Maw in one house and Paw in another. Built them, tore them down; tore them down and rebuilt them—fireplaces. Studied them. Studied their remnants. Smoldering cellar holes. With the intact chimney and fireplace. The handiwork of the short-cut artists. *And them what reckoned there warent nuthin to it.* The intact chimney with the creosote slathered on the outside of it, the side from which the fire jumped into the house structure. Sometimes that intact chimney speaks volumes. All kinds of things speak volumes to me.

Like the walls hereabouts. These here walls. Speak of a war. A war of seemingly endless skirmishes carried on over a period of close to forty years. A war that pitted father against son. The war is over now. The combatants have left the scene. I read its history, the history of its battles, just about every time I go to work on something. The father at rest now after a long, feisty, eventful life of ninety-plus years. And the son? Ah, the son. The issue at hand. Out there, I say, pointing towards the bay. Somewhere out there. He'll be the first; the first to swim the Atlantic, I joke. Sure to wash up any day now at Normandy. Just you watch. A strong distance swimmer, truly. One of those swimmers who won't win any races, but can go on and on and on. A residual skill from a childhood spent out here. Surrounded by water. Choppy salt water. Wherein be monsters. My other lame joke. Joined the food chain, I say to the fish-heads who knew him, who remember him from way back. "Chum at last," and they laugh a deep, coughing, cigarette-lung laugh; say to the few who are still around from back then, those guys who answer a greeting with, "I'm alive, I'm not in jail. It's a good day," and I wince now. So many things make me wince now. *I'm alive, I'm not in jail. I'm alive, I'm not in jail.* It can rattle around in my head for hours. Is it a good day? It is, of course. I notice tiny, extraordinary things; ordinary things that come to seem extraordinary, even through my exhaustion, as they say the condemned man will, and then it is a good day. An unbelievably, miraculously good day. Watching the little one with her mom does it for me damn near anytime. Like when they were hanging up laundry together yesterday, and she was trying to hold a piece of clothing under her chin like her mom does while clipping it on the line. No, it doesn't take much. Makes me go all to pieces.

Now Senior, he won races. And diving competitions. The old girl has some scalloped-edged black and whites from back in the day. A regular Tarzan was Senior, with his long, lean, athletic, muscular build, thick wavy hair that he carried with him all his days until it was a snow-white lion's mane, pencil-thin moustache he also took with him to the grave, though it was a little cockeyed there towards the end. A swimmer's build, but muscular too. Tarzan plus Rhett Butler. Must've been quite a catch in his day for the little— Here I stop myself, for who knows when this will come to light and who will read it? She certainly. My dear Ellen. She'll feel obliged to. That saddens me. I'll have to try to go easy on her mother. I'll also have to try to make this mess somewhat neat and tidy. Maybe give it a spiffy title. Preferably something that reeks with irony. Instead of this hideous, endless scrawl. Which merely reeks. Perhaps I've lost the reading public already. What else is left to lose?

I'll find out soon enough. Soon this will be all over. The men will be here for me, and this little interlude will be history. This little reprieve. Here's what I know about the commercial fishing out here, by the way: *cawd, haddawk*. They work the canyons and beyond with hooks for tuna and swordfish. They net bunkers for cat food. Smaller boats work the bays and inlets for shellfish, *lawbstuhs*. Then there are the charter boats for tourists and honeymooners and all the weekend warriors. That's all I know about it. After six-plus years out here that's all I know, and that all may be laughably incomplete or flat-out wrong. That's all I know about what goes on offshore. What built the island. A cute expression—what built the island. Something out of a real estate brochure or an information booth pamphlet. What built the island was a great big block of ice. A god-sized sand and gravel conveyor. With some hefty boulders sprinkled in. What builds the islands now besides delusions and self-delusions? Another day in paradise, we all say, trotting out the old cliché, showing up on a job site bleary-eyed at seven a.m. or so. I don't know what the fish-heads say when they get on the boats. I've never been on the boats. Junior was on one of the boats for a while in his youth. Didn't last too long. One of a string of washouts. Shark Bait they named him, and then just Chum. Chum. Kind of says it all. Kind of ironic, too, that I never got out on the boats given that I love to fish, or used to. I got busy. Fast. And never really had money to burn for a boat. Not the kind of money that a boat burns. We go out in the dinghy here in the harbor pond once in a while. Family outings. Good for the soul. The water's a little dirty—you can see a diesel slick or two and smell the exhaust. Some of the boats still empty their bilge out there. Ripens the estuary.

Delusions of earthly paradise; that's what builds the island. And every year less affordable and less like paradise. Back when it was the way people imagine it to be, almost anyone could afford a place out here. Now, to paraphrase the master, nobody can afford to come here anymore; it's too crowded.

I know where to bury this when the time comes, assuming it amounts to anything, which is looking increasingly unlikely. Lots of buried work in masonry. Walls behind walls. Backing work. Ballast. Mass. Support. Structural integrity. Buried work. Buried pieces of work. More inadvertent humor. More irony. What do I know for sure, after all? Perhaps he's still out there among the pines and oaks. Roasting cats. His phrase. Let them live behind the bus depot in cardboard boxes. Let them roast cats for dinner. That will get the cocky smirks off their faces. The Tacos, he meant. The Beaners. His Josés. Could really turn a phrase, could Junior. Had a way with words. Roast cats. Golden Geese clients. Your number one, triple A prime, *drop-everything-and-just-say-yes* clients. Golden geese. A rare breed. Inevitably old money. None of these bright-eyed newcomers quite made the cut. They're Avis clients at best—Wannabees usually. Junior's categories were rigid; nobody ever made it out of one and climbed into the next. We were all born into one of Junior's categories, apparently. Bet you never even knew it. More rigid than the British classes. More rigid than the Hindu castes. Golden Geese. Avis. Wannabees. All the contractors, whether local or off-island, what was his name for them? It was a gem. It'll come to me. He considered them little better than all the refugees who were washing up. Washed up. Never mind that he, himself had washed out repeatedly, but that's a different story. One that he was not reticent to share, by the way, given that it involved himself. A tale of injustice and ingratitude and injured innocence. A hero thwarted at every turn by lesser beings. Too bad he can no longer tell the tale. This will have to do. An inferior piece of work by an inferior piece of work. And such awful irony that I, who was supposed to be his protégé and became such a bitter disappointment, will have to be the one to tell it. Another in a long line of disappointments. Betrayers. He was beset by betrayers. And so he was forced into alliances and coalitions. His term again: coalition. Like OPEC. Like NATO. Dear Lord, it makes me giddy to think of it. And sad to think there's no one out there for him to assemble into a coalition. Only squirrels. My own incipient, insipid delusion, I know. Not so far gone yet.

I am directly responsible for his current status, his oneness with all and everything; his freedom, his peace, his cool, composed state. Let me get that out of the way, right out of the gate. Confession #2. Composed? Excellent. Composed state. Something like that. As for the other, my help, do we still cut off the right hand of the thief? Isn't that considered a touch old-fashioned? Barbaric? I believe he believed he was acting in self-defense. Call it delusion piled on delusion. They say the mind starts to break down after weeks and months of sleeplessness. Not for nothing is it considered torture. I have so far to go. So little time. The men will be here for me soon, any day now, and then this little interlude will be over.

2.

As I sit here before the hearth, before another fire, our sleepy little hamlet is in the midst of the annual St. Joe's day weekend festival featuring parade and continuous three-day blowout, hailed as the opening of the season, which, of course, it is anything but, the season being a full two months away, and, if you ask anybody who depends on it, closer to three, when the kids get out of school. More of a prolonged rain dance: wishful thinking, plenty of firewater, the virus of uncontrolled consumption on full display. The chant? The mantra? The prayer? That the Golden Geese will fly back, come home to roost for the summer, fertilize the island with their green, rich guano, then fly away again in early autumn. It works! The dance is done fervently enough every year, with enough gusto to fill sick beds and drunk pens and emergency rooms and pharmacies. The Golden Geese fly back. As do the Avises and Wannabees and tourists from around the world who fill the motels and inns and cottages to capacity for that brief, golden season. Junior didn't partake. I never saw him drink anything stronger than apple juice. He liked those little bottles of tea, flavored with fruit juice. In my time he never indulged in anything that might diminish his omnipotence.

Laughable as the notion may be—the contractor as demigod and legend in his own mind—it was far from unique to him. It was a syndrome; some would say a plague. Usually it afflicted those with more familiarity with controlled substances than he. With Junior the condition was endemic. And terminal. Really is laughable when you stop to think about it: builder as big shot. Not builders of cities. Not builders of monuments, cathedrals, great public works. No, builders of houses. Individual houses. Or sometimes just pieces thereof. Guys who, anywhere else in the country, anywhere else in the world, emerging as they do from the back of the classroom, then drifting into a humble life in the trades, rarely venturing far from home, while here, those same guys, their equivalent, entering into young adulthood directionless and adulthood without a profession, enter into a life in the trades and within a few years consider themselves major players, major actors on life's stage, ready to tick off the celebrities and self-styled big shots they've worked for and now fancy themselves, and then aren't they doing you a great big favor by even coming out to look at your job? They are, trust me, they are.

I pity the poor homeowners. I really do. Often as not, on meeting me for the first time, they'd say, "You returned our call!" And I: "I thought that's what you wanted." And they: "Yes, but contractors never return our calls." I returned their calls. I bid low. I was hungry. I had old debts to repay. I took any and all. At first. Bottom-feeder, the other builders called me. Warily. Others saw something. Like Junior, in whose orbit I at first found myself and under whose thumb I was supposed to be and remain. These builders have no idea how good they have it. If they're in their forties or younger, they've known nothing but boom times with a couple of slow years to catch their breath. More and more houses. Bigger and bigger houses, each more elaborate, more involved than the last. Never enough quality builders for the work, never mind the maintenance and repairs. And so the phenomenon of the prima donna contractor. The builder as rock star. I swear it's true. From spitball thrower to big shot. Homebuilder. Big shot. Mason. Big shot. Plumber. No, I'm not kidding. Again, I'm not talking about someone who's built a business and now has projects, crews, and offices all over. Talking about one guy with a few workers. A crew of two. Last summer I gave a ride to a young man, a college kid, who had to hitch-hike to get around. He was here for the summer from Eastern Europe, working at a couple of jobs, making tuition money.

"This place," he said, "not normal." Hit the nail on the head, buddy. You don't know the half of it.

Enter the illegals. In droves. *They* started showing up. *Them.* The aforementioned Tacos. And then the *'trabajo, dinero, cerveza'* contractors, local or otherwise, who make their living from them. \

Such unrelenting gloom this time of year. Junior had no use for the festivities, the excesses of the St. Joe's Day weekend. None of them did. Not Junior, not Senior, not the old bat, not Ellen or I. I was with Junior on that one. We saw eye to eye on many things. I to I. Let's see: overindulge in something that makes you stupid, then makes you sick, and if you stick with it long enough, will sap all your strength, ruin your life, and leave you a demented wreck. No, think I'll pass. He and I could go off on so many topics. As I say, he had no filters. He could be wonderfully amusing. Later he was just too medicated. Humor, by then, as often as not, was inadvertent and somewhat sad. He became thoroughly toxic. I was such a disappointment. Then a betrayer. Then a marked man. Others made fun of him behind his back. I did him the courtesy of laughing in his face. I was insufficiently sympathetic, insufficiently impressed. Insufficiently awed. Fatal flaws at least in one for whom he'd had such high expectations. He was just obliged to form that coalition against me.

That boil, for example. His Achilles boil. How was I supposed to keep a straight face? I know health problems are no laughing matter. I know that. Even after he had bragged ad nauseum that he had never lost a wallet and that he always kept his wallet in the same back right pants pocket, and I told him he had never lost it because he never took it out, except maybe to dust the money off once in a while and then put it back, which in itself was apparently not funny, and then to develop a boil on his butt, right under the same never-lost wallet, a boil that gets infected and lands him in the hospital. Not funny. I know that. Why'd he have to go on and on about it, though? As though the boil on his butt under the wallet that he had never lost was—well, there was just nothing in the world you wanted more to find out about. Asking for it. He was always like that. Seemed to revel in humiliation. It just got worse. Towards the end. There was time, though, I have to admit. In the course of the average day on a job site there was time to discuss Junior's boil. Junior's health in general. Became a whole special category. Anyone else might have health problems or injuries that got discussed in the usual way, but his—why, his were his. And anyway, whatever anyone else's problems, he could top it. He had you beat. He really did, too, after a certain point. A certain tipping point. *The medicated one.* St. Pete's phrase. St. Pete, who never made fun of anyone, who treated the most hard-luck, halfway-house cases on his job sites with the utmost courtesy and respect.

Dear St. Pete. It was an honor, sir. Sorry it had to end. What doesn't? That boil on Junior's butt was only one, was only the first in a long line of afflictions that take on, in retrospect, almost a Biblical aspect, so that if there are those still inclined to seek divine judgment in the afflictions of mankind or to mourn the seeming absence, the seeming departure of the wrathful, vengeful, Old

Testament Father from our day-to-day affairs they need only look to Junior's last few years for comfort and consolation, for reassurance. It's an ugly, primitive place for the mind to go, if you ask me, a desire we indulge whenever we say, "Couldn't have happened to a nicer guy," when something truly awful befalls someone we deem truly awful. Such accounts never tally. There is no justice in this life. "No end of laws and so little justice," as a wise man from another island once put it. Junior wasn't a monster anyway, and who can scrutinize his own reflection without a tinge of horror? Only a fool or a child.

My own child draws me away from this gallows gloom to take part in some outdoor games. Can I still smile? Dappled sunlight and a hint of warmth to the day. Windy, still windy. Always windy, but a hint of the coming spring. An easy winter. The land of perpetual autumn. Perpetual damp. Put a box of brand new envelopes in a desk drawer or filing cabinet, within a month they're all sealed shut. Ideal curing conditions. A mason's paradise. Welcome to paradise. This Edenic setting, this child's paradise: twelve acres of gently sloping lawns and lovely, sturdy cottages. The big house off to one side—a great cube. A great solid block, though tiny by the standards, the maxed-out standards of today. A solid colonial is the big house. Two full stories with an attic. Almost humble by today's standards. Nothing creepy about it either: no House of Usher, no Bates Hotel. Gray cedar shakes. Moderately pitched roof. An even, sensible pattern of double-hung windows. The reek of burning plastic emanating from the center flue chimney eight months a year. It stands there still to one side, respectfully, confidently minding its own business, as though ever ready to lend a hand, while seemingly serenely contemplating the harbor. The cottages, the kids, nearby. Sturdy and strong. We live in Number 2, the beautiful child. The 'L' on the harbor pond. A fireplace, a deck, two bedrooms. Big enough for our little family. Room to grow. Number 1? Vacant. Cluttered up with furniture and junk. The empty blockhouse style building. Number 1. Never got far from home, Number 1. Of the rest, six are rented full-time year round, four are at the moment vacant for one reason or another. Plus Number 1. Permanently vacant. The old lady still rattles around in the big house. She has an aide, the carry-over from Senior, Harold Sr., and his last few years. Ellen checks on her mom all the time. They go out together. Do errands, events. When the wind's right, or rather when the wind dies down, you can smell everything she's burning over there in the fireplace. Burns everything, does mother dearest. Burns all her garbage and junk mail in the fireplace. "I'm a burn bug," she says. "Mom's a burn bug," Junior used to say. Two sweet little peas in a pod they used to be. Two cute little scorpions in a bottle. I picture her in there, burning old tires, old roofing, two by fours with nails embedded and bits of sheetrock still attached, laying the sticks on the living room floor and feeding them into the fire little by little. The delusional vision of a feverish imagination.

Look at all the houses out here in our idyllic village—there are thousands. How many hundreds of them were built as a consequence, a direct consequence of one- and two-week visits to this place? Has to be hundreds. How many people—couples, young families—came out here and said, "This is it! Paradise found. We will buy; we will build." The old couple no doubt saw themselves as pioneers. Why should I sneer at that? They were pioneers in a way. They were way ahead of the crowd. They saw the crowd in; welcomed the crowd, the crowd coming as it does, not just from nearby cities and suburbs on the mainland but anywhere and everywhere you can imagine. If it seems paradise now, what must it have seemed then? Of course, it was rustic, deep country—fishing and farms and a long, bleak off season. But if you wanted a coastal summer getaway it was here for the asking.

Affordable summer cottages. Each one of those words on the mark. Cozy little cottages, by and large, back then, other than the handful of estates and mansions. Before our pioneers: fish-heads, rumrunners, the hearty leftovers from an earlier boom gone bust. Before that, three hundred years of the descendents of the original settlers creating with their own blood and sweat all that we take for granted during lives of hardship and tragedy. People with guts, brains. People who weren't afraid to get their hands dirty. Before that, three thousand years or more of a native people who hunted whales from dugout canoes and netted fish in the shallows, made their small settlements and burned the forests to improve the hunting and berrying and others who came to the island to do their burying and then went back to the mainland to their settlements, and before the Indians a windswept landscape of dunes and swamps and kettle holes and debris piles left by the melting glacial conveyor. Not that I know much about any of it. Beyond a point, beyond the Pilgrim settlers, there are few who know very much, the Indians having lived humbly and then lived and died humbly in service to the settlers. Lived and died humbly and in service.

Twelve acres on the harbor pond. Twelve acres on the harbor pond? How much? How much for the Gettysburg battlefield? How much for Boston Commons? Central Park? *No hay*. That's pronounced like 'I' for English-only purists. Not to be had. Pioneers. Believers. They came; others followed. The crowds came much later. This place, one extended, prolonged dance of a mature, loving couple. They were dancers, of course. Who wasn't, back then? Ballroom dancers. Prize-winners. They were mature; he in his forties, she in her late thirties by the time they moved here. They had some savings. They had sold their previous house to buy the land. He wasn't a builder. Some kind of finance career, then an officer in the Navy, then a few more years in a bank before the big move. Then lots of hacking and burning; and building. It's a neat thing about building: anybody can do it. There were manuals. Beyond that all you need is a brain, really. Half a brain. A certain tolerance for discomfort and pain. The stubbornness it takes to stick with something somewhat unpleasant and see it through. He was plenty stubborn, was Senior. Kind of a cranky old cuss. Well into his eighties by the time I met him. Anyone in his eighties has earned the right to be cranky, in my opinion.

I try to picture their early days out here: that lovely extended dance. A mature loving couple working together to create their world, their Eden. I'm sure they worked together—all ninety pounds of her next to her Tarzan. Her hero. They used what was available. No home supply superstore back then. There was a hardware store in town. A lumber yard on the other side of the island. They probably got a lot of their materials shipped directly from the mainland. You can still see the original oak sills and rough sawn framing lumber. *How* they built is more interesting to me than how they built. They had no architect; drew up no plans. On a construction site there's time. A construction site of one's own at least. Time to think. Time to imagine. To experience the place. To see, if you'll pardon the expression, where the building wants to go and what it wants to be. To let all the pieces, all the thoughts, all the questions and ideas swirl around unanswered until the lights come on. Like magic, that business. And hard wired. It's how our minds work, given half a chance. And in this case there was this lovely dance of husband and wife, mature, sure in each other, seeing eye to eye most of the time. I know what most husbands would say to that: she told him what to do and he did it. Not in this case. I knew that old boy. He was no pushover.

So they hacked away and burned and built one cottage: Number 2; the one we live in. They got it right. They nailed it. Then they built another: Number 1. The numbers have to do with the order in which you reach them along the entry drive and the proximity to the big house, I think. I'm still not sure. Then they built the big house. Then eleven more cottages, one through fourteen, skipping, of course, thirteen. I've heard the phrase often enough that it sounds like a cliché in my ears, though you'll almost never hear it in reference to the houses built out here recently, that they look like they grew out of the ground; like they're a part of their surroundings; like they belong. The cliché could have had its origin here. The whole place looks as at home in its setting as an African village or a compesino's farm. They got it right. Nothing fancy or complicated. Nothing pretentious. None of that slashing and burning was indiscriminate, for example. They left all those beautiful twisting shads and oaks and black pines and high-bush blueberries and beach plums—all those plants that make the native landscape such a feast for the eyes.

Feast for the eyes. Excellent. Back to the real estate brochure. The old couple added their own plantings, of course, tastefully, subtly; letting it all unfold year after year. Sprinkling the cottages between and around all these native plants, seemingly randomly, but on closer inspection, anything but. It's not as though you can't see one cottage from another. All those plants make for some privacy, but the cottages are in view of each other. It's just that each occupies such a distinct site they don't intrude upon one another. United but independent. Single story cottages except for Number 1, which is the only one that has that blocky feel; the only one that's kind of ugly, frankly. Other than the big house, only Numbers 2 and 5 are directly on the water, though they sit up as well, but since the whole site slopes gradually uphill almost all the cottages have at least a glimpse of the harbor.

Anyway, the water's there. Wherever you are on the property, walk a little, and you'll have a great view of the water. A beach, a dock, a dinghy for rowing, a tech dinghy and a sailfish for sailing. No cottage a carbon copy of any other. Their only contribution to the *max it out* philosophy is this last little row: 11, 12, and 14. I mean that jokingly, of course. Ironically, if you will. The place is anything but maxed out. This last row does look like a row. I'll grant it that.

These last three weren't built until the sixties, by which time old Harold, too, would have been in his sixties. Then there were repairs, additions, renovations. Construction is a young man's game. It takes its toll. My standard line about the work was that it's ninety-nine percent tedium and one percent excruciating pain. Over time the pain slice of the pie gets bigger. Assuming nothing catastrophic happens, you get about twenty-five years of actively doing the work. By then you're feeling it, so you need lots of help. Or you can move into management: tell a bunch of younger guys what to do. If you take care of yourself and have enough help you can keep at it until you're ninety-seven and can't remember which end of the tool is the handle. Old Harold was still banging away, still fixing, when I first came here for a visit, as I've mentioned, already well into his eighties. The little missus was still right out there with him. That's when I first got a sense of how they worked together. They were still dancing. It was beautiful to see. They needed help, obviously. Where was Junior? Living right there with them in the big house. How did Junior make his living? Construction. Hmm, let's see. This is a tough one.

Seems they couldn't quite work it out.

It was none of my business. I was just here for two weeks on vacation. Did more fishing in that two weeks, I think, than in the six-plus years I've lived here. The saying is that the local boys drop their hammers when the schools of blues and stripers show up. Given that there are always schools of something out there it's a wonder they ever pick up a hammer in the first place. Once I came here to work, there wasn't much time for fishing. If I wasn't working, I was recuperating. Okay, sleeping. Once she found out what I did for a living, it was the old gal who suggested I move here. "Come back. Lots of work. Live here." She always talked in clipped sentence fragments—still does—as if there just isn't time to speak in full sentences. She was always bustling; one thing to the next. Now she bustles more slowly. Spends more time in the living room of the big house looking out the big picture window towards the harbor. Having bustling memories. The last few years have been a trial: first Harold Senior's difficult decline, and now more recently—

Obviously, her suggestion must have lodged in my mind. It's a little difficult to reconstruct my reasoning back then, especially with everything else that's transpired. What must I have thought? What was I thinking? Ah, well, there's Ellen. And Liria. I try to cling to the positive.

This island, the idea of it, when you're on the mainland, when you're a builder on the mainland— just about wherever you are on the mainland—you know it's out there. You've heard of it. Heard stories. Rumors. It grows in your mind, in your imagination. Looms finally. Won't leave you alone. Takes on a sort of golden glow. The logic looks as plain as day. If you weigh the pros and cons, it looks like all pros; looks like the ultimate no-brainer. I, for example, had worked in two areas: the northern Rockies and interior northern New England, places where it's always too—something. Unless you find inside work, you're pretty much shut down four months a year. Here, by contrast, I could take outdoor jobs right through the winter. And money? Yes, there's money everywhere but here there's *Money*. How much money? Turn one of these pages on its side and write the word 'money' on it so that it covers the page. That's how much. And jobs going begging. And help. Good help. There's the thing. Never in twenty years could I consistently find good help. But here?—

Ah, good help. My right hand. My little red bull. The other issue at hand. More on that score soon enough. I think about Junior and the old couple even now, and I think it's a wonder they couldn't have worked something out. I think about their first fifteen or twenty years here—there were lots of lean ones. They had the property, a gorgeous property, but the point of owning property is not to be forced to sell it. Here the fifties and sixties were hardly boom times. So they were frugal. I've crawled around these places enough to know how old Harold did his building. I don't want to say he was a jury-rigger. He used what he had. He didn't waste wood, let's put it that way. If things sometimes seem a little cobbled together, they're sturdy enough. They're still standing. You can tell they didn't have money to burn. Plastic and cardboard and paper, yes. Money, no. So their expectation, their hope may have been that Junior's help would come at little expense. In short, that he'd be their slave. "Someday, son—" Which might have seemed a little unrealistic, a little unfair to poor Junior. A bit old-fashioned.

Like my little red bull, Catocho's first gig. With his father. Doing farm work from the age of four or five. For his tortillas and beans and a spot on the dirt floor to sleep at night with the vermin and the rats. And if you slack in your work and cry, you get stripes across your back and backside. More crying, more stripes. Tradition. Culture. Junior, whatever his shortcomings, was no fool. He was also a pretty fair builder when he wanted to be. His adulthood coincided with the boom years, which, once they started, have never really ended. Probably resented an arrangement that smacked of indentured servitude, that seemed a throwback to the Dark Ages, that involved payment to be received in full in, say, thirty years or so. Still, you'd think they could have worked something out instead of locking horns for twenty-five years.

I used to bring it up with Ellen once in a while. She'd wave me off. Oh, he was always like that. Always had a chip on his shoulder. (She didn't call him Junior. She'd say "Harold" through her nose, imitating his whiny, screechy voice.) He was a teenager by the time she remembers him, given their age difference. She was born out here. He came along for the ride. Slithered in. The most unlikely pair of full-blooded siblings imaginable. Also hard to imagine that you could grow up out here back then and be anything but a happy, well-adjusted kid; turn into anything but a happy, well-adjusted adult. They have a photo album from back then in the big house; some school pictures framed in the living room. He does look like he was a happy kid. Not a trace of that scowl, that snarling scowl he always wore, that *you'd-better-hope-your-face-doesn't-freeze-like-that* scowl. He was a good-looking kid, too. Can't imagine what happened there either. It must seem I'm trying to present him as some evil figure when most often, if you'd seen the two of us together you'd have sworn we were pals, chums. Catocho took to calling him *Demonio, Serpiente*. He had a habit of sending me scrambling for my Spanish-English dictionary—Catocho, not Junior, and not for those words but for others. He had such a ready store of proverbs and aphoristic pronouncements, like as not emanating from the Prophets. His was a decidedly Old Testament Christianity: full of fire and brimstone. His judgment of Junior had a far more emphatic, less ambiguous character than my own. To bring a lawsuit against his own parents! An abomination. Despicable, in Catocho's eyes. Unforgivable. I was inclined to agree. Junior had a long-running lawsuit against his parents. Pretty appalling. The thing never came to any kind of resolution. Lord knows what it cost them all. It was a torment to his folks, I knew, and a source of heartache for Ellen. To Catocho, it was simply an unforgivable offense. Capital. You honored and served and obeyed your parents. You didn't bring them grief and torment in their last years, much less bring lawsuits against them. Who can argue?

A neat little guy, my Catocho. Solid. Self-respecting. A nut-brown bowling ball. Maybe five feet tall. Maybe a hundred and twenty pounds. Soaking wet. Pound for pound the best worker I've ever laid eyes on. My right hand, and in the end, both hands. And in the end—

Junior had an ongoing lawsuit with his folks and kept right on living there in the big house with them, sleeping in his old childhood bedroom. The suit was ongoing when I got here and went on. Until the end. Without resolution. Must have cost them all a fortune. He didn't even drop it after the old man died. Felt like I'd dropped into a war zone. Plenty awkward. This paradise on earth was a regular nest of vipers. I thought about cutting out that first fall and winter—the whole first year, actually. At that time Ellen was still with her firm on the mainland. I was already in debt to the old gal. I was to work off my rent. That was the deal. They'd get their repairs done, and I'd have a roof over my head. I'd give her a week of time per month in exchange for the use of a cottage. Fourteen. The cottage I'm sitting in at the moment before the smoldering fire.

That's all she said when I got here: "Fourteen." Then, I guess I looked a little puzzled. I just stood there. "You stay in Number 14," she explained, enunciating each word clearly and speaking a little louder as though she were dealing with a particularly dim four-year-old, then shook her head and bustled off. The next time I saw her she had another one-word pronouncement: "Skirting." That must have left me looking really stupid. "We're closing in under the cottages; winterizing. Skip will show you." More overly loud words. More shakes of the head. Skip was her pet name for Junior. Nobody else called him that. By the time I called him anything, I called him Junior. That debt I managed to get into with the old lady: my old Nissan truck crapped out that fall. She loaned me half of the six grand I needed to buy my F-150, which was only a few years old at the time. I think I'm still paying for it, though it's long since been squashed into a cube, shipped to China and made into—something. Quite a shrewd operator was the old gal.

You learn a lot about places when you spend a month crawling around underneath them. By the time I moved here, years after that fishing vacation, old Harold was still roaming the grounds, though he no longer did any repairs. He was starting to show signs of the condition that would hit full force the next year. Junior latched right onto me. Thought he'd found a kindred spirit. Someone else who liked crawling around under the cottages. A protégé. Instant best friend. Who knows what he thought? The mind recoils. He went on and on about the lawsuit: ongoing, pending, *blah-di-blah*. He wanted his cut it seems; his half of the property or the value thereof. How was it his? In what sense his? Got me. Excellent questions.

3.

I like this Number 14. Out of the way here. Just a little box of a place. Cozy. The poor cousin on the property. Ellen practices her oboe and clarinet in here, which, I inform her, draws in the stray cats, and she is amused but just barely. This property, these cottages, their configuration, relation, relation to the land, its trees, the harbor, the broader surroundings—which is nothing less than the visible, tangible expression of the lifelong and eternal love between two people, their interplay, the dance of their thoughts and dreams, around which the last fifty years of their life together was built, revolved—

And he wanted his cut. It wouldn't do. Outmoded. Old-fashioned. Wasted land. Wasted space. Why, half the property was unused. *Half.* Did I know that? Nature walk they called it. Isn't there enough open land out here? Did I know how many building lots there were on this property? And what those lots were worth on the open market today? Sure, Junior. Whatever you say. So he sued them. Wanted his cut. Must have driven him nuts. Must have made him eat his liver. Here we were—we!— winterizing these old places so they could be rented year round, when one building lot—*One!* He'd go on like that and in any number of variations on the same theme.

His lawsuit was his favorite topic at first. Later on it became his health: his boil on his butt, his Lyme, his Hep C. His, his, his. I, I, I. Nor was I the only one he treated to these dissertations. He'd blather on about his lawsuit with the delivery guy from the lumber yard and the mailman and the meter reader. Like he was stamping the word *LOSER* on his forehead in great big letters. Initially at least I wasn't quite so blatant; so blatantly contemptuous. I ventured to ask in my most awe-shucks, Montana-ranch-boy tone, just whose name was on the deed? Perhaps he had an early sense of mutiny, insubordination. Turned all purple in the face. That wasn't the point. No, apparently not. I, I, Junior.

By the way, the fact that the cottages could be rented year round and for good rates showed how things had changed. Forty years ago they could barely rent them during the summer. The skirting was one of those 'first job in the area' kind of jobs. Not exactly interesting or challenging. The kind of job established contractors passed on. Passed off. I had a lot of those. In this case I would make two-by-four frames, attach pressure-treated plywood to the exterior and insulation covered with plastic sheeting stapled to the interior, then attach them under the perimeter of the cottages. Of course, the perimeter of the cottages had all kinds of stuff in the way: plant beds, trees, decks, fuel tanks. Lots of crawling around with drop lights. There were usually at least a couple of feet of clearance. Not too many hazards. Dry ground. Often pure sand. Okay, impure sand to be more precise. The strays in the neighborhood had found all that sand. There are lots of strays around. People leave them when they move away. Underneath these things is apparently where lots of animals chose to end their days. Little wildlife hospices. I made a collection of all the skulls—not just cats: possums, raccoons, skunks. One goat. Don't ask me. Maybe it was Junior's. Must have smelled great under there for a month or two. They were setting up propane furnaces more or less at the same time, bolting them to the underside of the floor joists, so there was all that flexible duct work to work around. It wasn't a bad job, really, beyond the cat box reek, the skulls. Lots of construction jobs are like that: just put in your day and try to enjoy the view of the harbor once in a while. Zero stress. Sure it's boring, but that's the way the work is: when it ceases to be life-threatening, it immediately becomes boring.

Life-threatening. Truly is a pity Junior started trying to kill me. Maybe he was just trying to scare me. We'll never know. Crawling around under these places, I started to get a feel for how they're built: sturdy, strong, ad hoc, a little cobbled together but not going anywhere. The old man wasn't a builder so he did what a smart amateur does when he's unsure: overbuild. Lots of piers—posts of some kind of masonry for foundations. Short spans. Some kind of masonry and any kind of masonry, which is fine. The compressive strength of concrete is such that it can hold ten times the building it typically carries. No earthquakes around here to speak of. At least not lately. Just wind. Lots of wind. Not good if the cottage flops off the foundation piers. He had these things bolted and strapped down long before that was required. The masonry might include anything and everything from flue tiles filled with concrete to beach bricks and flagstones. Beach bricks are bricks or brick pieces or whole chunks of brick walls that have somehow fallen into the ocean, gotten scoured around for a few years, then washed ashore. Ellen and I collect them. For the hearth I'll never have a chance to build.

You could see Junior's handiwork under the cottages too—where he'd stepped in to show old Dad how it was done. Often where he'd stepped in and then stepped out before finishing the job. There are far too many amateur shrinks around these days. Too many people feel qualified to chime in as to what makes somebody else tick. More people should mind their own business. Junior was just such a blatant piece of work you couldn't resist. Just couldn't help yourself. There was old Harold, Senior: Tarzan in his youth, long and lean, champion swimmer, diver, dancer; successful in banking when banks were failing by the thousands, successful in the Navy—helped defeat Tojo in the Pacific, moved out here to become a pioneer, hacking this place out of the wilderness and building it up with his bare hands, little woman by his side. There he was, still at it: fixing the old places up well into his eighties, still handsome, strong, virile; thick wavy white hair, crooked little moustache.

And Junior? With that stooped gait and dumpy build and those woggly eyes that never quite looked at you and that tangled-up beard that looked like every hair was doing its best to get as far as possible from every other hair, that whiny, screechy voice, that big round goofy-looking bald spot; washed out of the Navy and washed out of the Merchant Marines and then couldn't make it on a commercial boat where they called him *Chum* in honor of the crap you threw overboard to attract sharks—Chum, not even Bait. Then failed with his own charter boat and so ended up doing construction and never amounted to much at that either. Living at home with his mommy and daddy in his old bedroom in his fifties. Used up before he ever got started. It didn't take a genius. Sorry, Dr. Freud, your services will not be needed. A pipsqueak in the shadow of a giant his whole life. You had to feel sorry for him. I always did. In my own sick way. Catocho never liked him. Never felt sorry for him. *Strange*, he'd say. "He strange. Very different." Hit the nail on the head, amigo. Can't argue with you. I had found certain things amiss while crawling around under these places. Other than animal skulls. Call it things out of place. Call it evidence. Evidence of strangeness at the very least. Gave me pause. Even that early on.

Catocho was there working on the grounds, too. Not working directly for the old couple. He was with the company that did some of the grounds work. The first time I saw him they were putting the irrigation to bed, draining the lines. Amazing how quickly, instantaneously even, some partnerships are formed. I took one look at him: that squashed, solid build. No neck to speak of. Nut-brown face. "What part of the Highlands you from?" I asked. I had guessed Verapaz and wasn't far wrong. He beamed and clapped me a solid handshake. "I work for you," he said. Left me with something else to think about. By then with almost twenty years in construction almost equally divided between building small, beautiful homes with Boss Haas in Colorado and working on my own in New England and through all that time there was one constant: not enough help, undependable help, help that thought it was partner inside of a week, help that tried to turn itself into the competition inside of a few months. Year after year of three-man jobs done with a little help around the margins and two-man jobs done alone. In fact, that was what I could count on: help that I couldn't count on. I gave him my number. Told him to call when they got laid off. Meanwhile the skirting was coming along. They wanted two roofs reshingled next, hopefully before the winter; hopefully the last two roofs I'll ever reshingle. A mild year, right through the winter, like the one just past. Brand new millennium. "Will the Internet devour the universe?" I ask the various gurus, financial or technological, I come across. They laugh. Talk of a needed correction. Used to be that a high-school teacher who watched his or her pennies could eventually afford a summer cottage out here; spend vacations at the beach. Now some of the couples buying ten thousand square-foot mansions look like high-school students. Ah, well. A correction. Things out of plumb, out of level. Just a scosh. And soon to come: free, instantaneous communication from anywhere on earth to anywhere else on earth. Something else new under the sun. What's that, Your Majesty? They're all just saying the same dumb things? Can't have everything. I say, more power to the people of the zeroes and ones, the golden prophets of oneness, demonstrating yet again the harmony of numbers, in this case leading to bank accounts uncountable. St. Pete was such an entrepreneur, though no high-school student.

The roofing jobs, first Number 1, then 7, took twice as long as necessary thanks to Junior's supervision; subversion. And I had given his mom a price, a time estimate, which she did not forget and which she did not treat as an estimate. Two peas in a pod, those two. Likes round numbers, she says, any time she has to pay for something, and rounds down. Both roofs were about the same: the surface layer looked horrible—all curled edges and broken shingles, but underneath was a layer of roll roofing tarred completely to the roof boards. That old man was no fool. Through forty years of gales and salt wind that layer hadn't budged or degraded. No leaks either, as far as I could tell. Oh no, said Junior. Take it down to the roof boards. I'm a perfectionist, said Junior. His reasoning was a little obscure. There was no scraping that layer off. It had to be chiseled off with sharp cold chisels. This by way of illustration. I had landed between the scorpions in the bottle, and while I did my best to avoid that situation—never again giving the old gal a time estimate, for example—the situation recurred with some regularity. She and Junior seemed to work out a system whereby he'd inherit me to get some of his own contract jobs done.

I had already placed an ad in the island newspaper, and I immediately started getting calls, so it was becoming obvious that once I got off those roofs I'd get some paying work. I bid low. I returned calls. Bottom-feeding. Call it what you will. Some of those calls were from contractors, and it was pretty obvious that some of those relationships would eventually pay off no matter what I earned initially. Lots of small jobs and repairs were going begging. What did I care if they were unglamorous repair jobs? As if construction jobs are supposed to be glamorous. Repair jobs are fun. You're done within a week or two, usually. You take some broken-down, useless entry paving or patio or crumbling chimney or cracked foundation and leave it all spiffed up and back in service.

4.

I had to take all the jobs I could. I had to keep Catocho happy. The man devoured work. The man did not want down time. In fact, I couldn't keep him busy that first winter. I only had a couple of jobs on which I could use him, but the next spring, once he'd committed to working for me, it sunk in. When I say he didn't want down time, I mean days off. Ever. Other than Sundays. Here was something new. As novel to me as the Internet and even more remarkable. "I love my work," he said to me on more than one occasion, slowly, emphasizing each word, when he thought I might be having doubts about his loyalty or ability or just losing interest in generating enough jobs to keep him employed. He loved his work, and in those few words, carefully and slowly enunciated—what wasn't he saying? He loved my work. He loved working for me. He was saying everything that a man such as he could express and in a manner as eloquent in its own way as I'd ever heard it expressed. How could I turn my back on him?

If I had six days of work for him every week, he was happy. Five he could tolerate. Four and he would have left, would have gone back with one of the landscapers or tried to catch on with another builder. Overtime pay? Give me a break. Not until St. Pete took us both on. Many weeks that first full year he made more than I did. I often had to ask myself who worked for who. So many of the jobs I took were to keep him in work. How he burned through it. He particularly loved long days of hard physical labor. Loved it. I'd never seen anything like it. I puzzled over what was wrong on one of our first little jobs—we were repointing some brick work—so I asked him. "We're doing so little. Will they actually pay us?" he asked. Ah. Let me worry about that. My problem. They do pay, eventually. Usually. The work wasn't hard enough. That was the problem. He couldn't get enough work, and he loved best work that was most difficult physically, no matter how tedious. Something new, indeed. I merely had to list the tasks to be done, and they were done in the order they were listed or the order specified. Unheard of. A little genie of physical labor. A genius of physical labor. Don't worry, I'm not saying he was a genius. He wasn't raised to solve complex equations or puzzles or to be inventive or studious or even curious—that in itself no small irony given his ancestors', his people's achievements. He was raised to do exactly as his immediate forbears had done: to toil on the land and toil for outsiders when the need or occasion arose, seasonally. Their own planting and cultivating and reaping and that of others, for a little cash, for as long as anyone where he comes from could remember, and if a diet such as he'd grown up on, consisting chiefly of corn and salt, makes for a virtual certainty that a child will never have much capacity for solving complex equations or sustained inquiry, but will instead develop an aptitude, a brilliance for that which he was trained with a switch across his back from the earliest age, what was it but more evidence of the order of things?

Catocho was in no sense a rebel, in no sense a disrupter of the order of things. His detours in life from that which anyone in his family had done before had come in service to and often at the behest of the elders, for seasonal labor, whether farm labor or anything else, is done for a little money, and when you work for a little money, you go where there's more of it. We often had to drive posts, usually sharpened two-by-fours, using an eight- or ten-pound maul to hold plywood in place to protect our narrow excavations; in short, to keep from burying ourselves, and I would hold the posts from down in the excavation and on occasion I would look up as he swung hard and hit the top of the post and never missed. I could have put my head within a few inches of the top of the posts and not sustained a scratch, and I would wonder how he did that. How he never missed. So I asked him, and he said that his first paying job was working on the road, call it a highway, though it's at best a two-lane road they'd been working on, apparently, forever, entirely by hand, entirely without machines. There were ledges and boulders that they would split using sledges and chisels, one man holding the chisel, the other driving it in until the fissure held it. "You learn to never miss," he said. This for a dollar a day. Then came a stint in the army, the regular army, also for about a dollar a day, plus room and board, room meaning, more often than not, a tent or a trench while on patrol in the countryside, digging trenches that his life depended on; getting ambushed; seeing his buddies get shot to pieces.

We had about half a dozen different mixes depending on what we were doing, plus, call it another half a dozen variations, all of which we mixed on site in a small electric mixer. He never botched it. In five years he never botched a batch. He must have, of course. I just can't think of a time; that's how rare it was. You can fix a batch, but he rarely had to do that either. Most often we worked in close proximity, so I could see him there mixing away. Very rarely did he have to add a little of this or that once the mix was in the wheelbarrow. I imagine you'd have to be a tender for a while, at least a month or two, to realize that's not so easy. I can't dwell on it at the moment. It turns out, on his way north after his stint in the army, he had made a detour and worked on the high rises going up on the beach in Cancun. Spent most of a year there making two, three, eventually four dollars a day mixing concrete in troughs with hand tools. If you could mix precisely and consistently, your pay was increased accordingly until, in his case, it was almost on a par with the masons. But even the masons made only a little more, so the hotels on the beach were only a detour on the journey north.

At that time they snuck into the States through a hole in the fence in Brownsville or Laredo, then by van to enormous farms and food processing plants all over the country, then, in his case and apparently in the case of most others, back through the fence later the same year, since the work was seasonal and there was seasonal work to be done at home as well, not to mention time to rest and be with family. That's how it went for a few years, migrating from home to the melon fields and citrus groves of Florida, then back home again. After that he didn't dare leave. Immigration was getting more vigilant on this side, and the other side was increasingly controlled by drug-runners, thieves, rapists, content to take what they could from the migrants, then dump them in the desert to roast. He applied for asylum. He had a case. He had received death threats back home. It was a stretch, though not a flat-out fabrication. It went back to his army days. It wasn't likely to fly, but they gave him some kind of provisional status and a card to prove it. As long as he filed his taxes and proved that he was employed, which he did promptly and proudly and without fail. He showed me all the forms and returns and complained about the taxes, not nearly as much as the rest of us complained about our taxes. Just enough to show that he had joined the club. That he was quasi-legal. My quasi-legal tender. So the phrase 'genius of physical labor' might seem every bit as oxymoronic as the phrase 'big-shot mason' or 'big-shot plumber,' but it was an extremely meaningful phrase to me.

He lived in a trailer on the far side of the island—there's a small trailer park over there in the woods between Sterling and Ponnack Harbor, next to a large stretch of protected woods—he and his wife and sister-in-law and about half a dozen of their countrymen, so he usually had about a twenty-minute or half-hour commute to our job sites, which tended to be closer to here. He always beat me to the job site in the morning—almost always— often by ten or fifteen minutes. He showed up on our first full job in an overcoat about ten sizes too large; a pink, down-filled parka that some Nordic Amazon must have donated to Goodwill. It reached his calves, and he had to tape back the sleeves. What did he care how he looked? He had work. He was warm. Most of his housemates and co-workers from the landscape company were huddled in their homes wondering how they were going to make it through the winter, much less send money home to relatives. Our job was at about the highest point on this side of the island, the uppermost house in a development called Hilltop Estates—developers are such poets—doing flat exterior work. January and into February. Stiff winds. Relentless stiff winds. Many mornings I envied him that pink parka. Wanted to wrestle him for it. He was all business. Didn't want to talk about his parka or anything else. *What do I do?* And then, finishing that task, *What do I do now?* I offered him breaks. Repeatedly. He had no interest in breaks. Twenty minutes, maybe a half hour for lunch, usually after finishing one task and before starting another. That's how he worked, all day, every day. For five years. Until last year about this time.

That first job was a good one for me to land early on, coming as it did directly from my little ad and not through Junior or another contractor, since it involved intricately laid brickwork on full slabs; one a curved, herringbone-pattern walkway, the other a broadly curving patio, each with stairs of brick risers with bluestone treads leading up to, in the one case, the front entry, and in the other, the side deck. There was a lot of cutting involved, both for the edging soldier course around the curves and all the bricks that met the edging and, in the case of the curving herringbone walkway, many of the field bricks as well, since I was a stickler about keeping the joint width uniform. I sensed this homeowner might not particularly care about some of the finer points, but I wanted to be able to show people the job or at least direct them to it. As an example it proved useful. We nailed it. The front walk, in particular, had the potential to be a train wreck, but laying it out dry and admittedly doing a couple of sections twice, it became something I could confidently point to. Catocho gamely managed the wet saw and showed no impatience with having to recut bricks I deemed a little too sloppy. I'd mark; he'd cut. As long as I kept marking, he kept cutting. When I got a sense that he tended to take off a little too much, I just started nudging my marks over by an eighth inch or so. I set the miscuts aside and ended up using most of them somewhere else on the same job. We wasted a few bricks, but bricks are relatively cheap in the scheme of things, even those pretty rosy-hued ones we were using. Daytime temperatures usually hovered around freezing, and the wind seemed to never let up, but he didn't seem to consider the work any great hardship. It wasn't, generally. At least that was the approach I tried to take. The job was no picnic. It was nothing special. You did it and went home and went to bed and kept coming back until it was done.

About two weeks into it, he arrived long after I did one morning, which, as I've mentioned, was a rarity. In five years it was a rarity. When he arrived he was shaking, visibly shaking from head to toe. It turned out, of course, that he wouldn't have been late at all; in fact, he'd anticipated getting to the job especially early to have things all set up when I arrived. The day had the potential to see us complete a major chunk of the brickwork and he wanted to do all that he could to see that it happened. So he was in a bit of a hurry, passed a town truck, which for some reason was poking along, and got stopped. The cop got him for two moving violations plus something to do with his insurance card. Probably just toting around the expired one as happens half the time with me. None of that explains why he was standing in front of me shaking like a leaf. He thought I might fire him. Once he was done thinking that this town cop had the authority to revoke his quasi-legal status, take him in and have him deported immediately, he thought he'd get to the job site, and I'd fire him for being a little late. I don't remember if I laughed. I know I left him with the impression that we don't get bent out of shape about such things. Needless to say, when his court date came around, I helped him get the violations reduced so that his insurance wouldn't go up. I still see him standing there in front of me shaking from head to foot, afraid I'd fire him because he was an hour late because a cop was bored in the off season.

Some of us joke that in the off season we each have a cop assigned to us. That's just how it seems sometimes. Now the joke's on me. Soon, perhaps, I get a whole shift. That aside, I'm reminded of another tiny incident that occurred that winter. Catocho was in the truck with me while I did some running around. Among my errands was going to the bank. No doubt I was withdrawing money. I wasn't depositing much at that point. One of the jokey things I often say is, I'm off to rob the bank. If I'm talking to Ellen, say, about a banking errand, I'll say, I'm off to rob the bank. Need any money? That kind of thing. So that morning I said to Catocho, "Today we rob the bank," as though I were announcing the day's job. "That's fine," he said. No, "Ha, ha." No, "Great, get me a million." Just, "That's fine." So I looked over at him, and he was looking ahead at the road as if what I'd just said was, say, "—and now to the supply yard." Just as serious as ever. Kind of scared me.

I didn't have any other work for him that winter. Needless to say, I didn't want to lose him. I wasn't in a position to just keep him busy doing things here at the cottages. I couldn't afford to even if I'd wanted to. Junior and the old lady weren't about to hire him for my sake. He understood. We'd work together again starting in the spring. That gave me time to line up more work; to get my own business up to code.

All during that brick job it had bothered me that I'd lost my hammer, a regular twenty-dollar mason's hammer, but I'd had the thing since I'd started working. When we cleaned up the job site, there it was under the sand tarp, under the ground tarp. I asked him about it. He thought he'd seen something as he lay down the tarp, but hadn't stopped to notice what it was. It had been windy. Moreover, he'd been following my instructions. Precisely. And in the order given. Ah.

Almost makes me giddy now to think of it in these terms. His was a decidedly Old Testament Christianity and in some perverse way he'd end up helping turn me into a New Testament Christian: in the end I merely had to think something to become guilty of it.

Chapter Two

"That Which You Seek
Is All Around You."

1.

*W*HEN I CAME OUT HERE on that fishing vacation all those years ago, about the first thing that caught my eye was the stairway to nowhere. That just came to be my name for it, obviously: the stairway to the second floor deck and main entrance to Cottage Number 1, which by then was just a storage building for Junior's things; an annex to his lair. It was missing the bottom three feet, this stairway, its last five or six treads, so it didn't quite make it to the ground. I guess my nickname was a bit off, a bit bass ackwords, but it had a nice ring to it, so I stuck with it. Junior had a stepladder propped against it, for whenever he needed to get in there, to add or subtract. When I came here to live—whatever it was—almost four years later, that gravity-defying, metaphysics-inducing stairway was still the first thing that caught my eye when I drove in. Maybe it was a different stepladder. But I doubt it.

I mention it now because it occurs to me that I've brought up this war between the generations, this tempest in a teapot and, at least in relation to the ways it manifested itself in repair projects around the cottages, I've provided inexcusably little evidence. And there it was, Exhibit A, staring them, me, anybody, right in the face as you drove in. The story immediately becomes tedious in the retelling, but that's the nature of construction work, the nature of the beast: tedious. Build and tear something apart five times, it's a tedious business every time. I should also hasten to add that in any sprawling complex of homemade construction such as this, particularly one in which budgets and labor are limited, there are bound to be repair projects that go begging, essentially, forever. In itself it was nothing extraordinary or peculiar. Given its prominence in a place where appearances seem to be so important, one might think that doing something about it might become a priority. I can applaud them for that, for not caring what other people thought, except it wasn't true; they did care what other people thought. Even Junior, in his own sick way. And given that I heard the story repeatedly and in every version and from every angle, I think I can state with some authority that there wasn't much to praise in how this permanent eyesore came to be. (I fixed the thing, by the way, early in the spring of my first year out here, and there wasn't much to praise, much heroism, in that either.)

The stairway was built from whatever framing lumber the old man had available back in the fifties, so it shouldn't be too surprising that, thirty-some years later it was a little worse for wear. So it makes

it to the top of the old man's list, eventually—
bubbles up—they'll fix that old stairway; start to get
Number 1 back into shape for rental. So he totes out
his sawhorses, his handsaw and hammer, his rusted
coffee tins filled with straightened used nails of
sizes ten, twelve, and sixteen penny, his scraps of
framing lumber—probably the same stuff he'd used
to build it. And so he revs up the old handsaw and
starts whaling away on those rotten stringers. He'll
cut off those stringers about waist high to get rid of
the rot down near the ground, make clean, level
cuts, then scab on new pieces, double them up and
nail the daylights out of them. I have no doubt he
would've had the new treads back on the next day;
maybe that same afternoon. You really had to
admire the old boy.

He gets as far as cutting off the stringers. Then
Junior comes along. To save the day / put a halt to
the proceedings. (To save the day—slash—throw a
spanner in the works.) What the old man was doing
wasn't up to code; they'd get their asses sued. He'd
take the project on. Take it over. Tear out the old
stairway completely and start over. Pressure treated
lumber; poured concrete footings with anchor bolts.
(Complete overkill, by the way, that last part. Old
Harold had a couple of blocks buried in the sand for
the footing.) Anyway, this is where things get a little
strange; a little surreal. They'll have to sub out the
last part: the excavation, the concrete, since Junior
can't be expected to do it, and anybody the old lady
tries to hire for the job doesn't measure up to
Junior's standards; just won't do. A very exacting
business, apparently, pouring a little footing for a
set of outdoor stairs. He chases them off one after
another.

So there the project sat in plain view for the world to see, for however many years until my first spring out here. By which time Harold Senior was pretty much out of the picture, at least as far as repairs went. Left unstated was Junior's agenda in leaving the stairway unrepaired, which is to say he liked the building just fine as an annex to his lair and had no intention of seeing it put back into service as a rental cottage. Again, I merely go into such detail to provide a glimpse of how things operated, how things had evolved. What house doesn't have projects going begging?

These examples of the construction battlefield are all around me. But they're tedious. And individually, they look like nothing in particular. Anyway, there isn't time. And the jury has limited use and patience for such details. It was only in the aggregate that they came to look like something kind of—awful—and it took some time before I got the picture myself.

There was another project that ended up on my 'to-do' list early in that first spring here, which comes to mind because it sheds a little light on another facet of Junior's nature. Unfortunately, the project also sheds a little light on my nature, but there's no avoiding it. It comes back later on in the narrative, this tendency of mine, if the narrative makes it that far. I can be stubborn. Okay, pig-headed. Another confession. Confession #3, I think. Taken to the extremes that I can take it, this can come to seem the grossest stupidity, though I'll choose to believe it illustrates no such thing.

The project was taking down a tree, a white pine, which must have planted itself some time early in the 1900s, or, at any rate, long before our settlers arrived. White pines aren't the predominant pine out here, but they do occur. And they're planted. This pine had attained impressive girth. It really was a beautiful tree: enormous, sweeping limbs, picturesque double top. Character. I could see why the old couple had liked it, had left it out there at the edge of the woods just beyond the cottages, standing about ten feet above high tide. That's the way they'd done things: they had a genuine sense of relaxed, natural-looking landscape beauty. Unfortunately, this beautiful old tree had seen better days; maybe too much of its root system had reached salt water. Big chunks of bark had fallen off; a number of limbs were dead or dying. All of which made it even more picturesque, by the way. It was a shame to have to take it down, but it had a distinct lean to the southeast and that meant that the wrong storm, the wrong twisting wind might take it down for them, taking out a couple of cottages along the way. Or at least that was the old couple's fear. I didn't think so; didn't think the tree would fall that way or reach the cottages no matter what, and told them so, but it was their call.

Taking down this tree was a job for climbers, or maybe a bucket truck, but the old couple's inclinations being what they were and mine being mine, the job ended up on my list. What got me into hot water in this case was volunteering the information to the old gal that a tree can often be persuaded to fall in the opposite direction from which it leans. It doesn't always work, even for guys who drop trees all day for a living, and it didn't work for me this time. After I'd made the notch and started the back cut, I drove in wedge after wedge behind the saw blade. By the time only a sliver of hinge of wood was left between the notch and the back cut, and the cut was full of wedges, it was pretty obvious: that tree was having none of it. It just wanted to fall toward the cottages, or at least the shoreline, the water, and not back towards the woods.

This was where my mule-headedness kicked in. Junior was handy, so I had him bring me an extension ladder, his longest chain, and his backhoe. I set the ladder up in the tree, got up in there as high as I could reach, and wrapped the chain around the biggest limb handy, got down and brought the other end of chain in the direction we wanted the tree to fall, dog-legged the chain around another tree so Junior's backhoe would stay out of harm's way, hooked on to his bucket and pulled for all that backhoe was worth. No dice. By the way, we've already entered crazy-land here. I had just leaned the ladder against a tree that was 95 percent cut through and climbed it to attach a chain to the tree. But it gets worse. In fact, what I decided to do at this point makes me shudder to recall it. I decided to get the weight distribution in our favor by climbing the ladder to the top again, this time with the chainsaw all lit up, and drop the biggest limb handy that leaned the wrong way. What I planned to do at that point is anybody's guess. Turn around and say, I told you I could do it, while I came crashing down with the tree, maybe.

I did stop myself. After I'd climbed the ladder again with the chain saw running. Maybe I envisioned the headline: 'Man commits one-of-a-kind suicide.' I got rid of the ladder, unhooked the chain from the backhoe and brought the tree down in the direction it leaned, harmlessly, with only a couple of extra hours of cleanup. It made quite a hop off the stump as I finished the cut from the notch side; a big splash as it flopped along the shoreline.

Junior comes into this in his absence. In absentia. He had given me the rope—the chain—to hang myself. He hung back. Took it all in. From a distance. He was taking notes. Taking note. And he didn't forget what he had learned. He put his knowledge to good use. Call it my imagination. Or maybe something of note for me alone. At this point I find it a fascinating sequence to call to mind, that's all.

2.

I know full well what the jury wants. The jury cries out for the evidence. Of his strangeness. Of his peculiar proclivities; inclinations. The jury fairly drools for it. And yet I don't oblige. Junior is not the one on trial here. Instead I take his part. If I go to some length to provide detail it's merely to put flesh on the bones—to put flesh back onto the bones—of a human being. He wasn't a monster. I flesh him out in pity, in nostalgia. He was my wife's brother. We all miss him. No, I won't indulge this particular craving. For dirt. Other than where absolutely necessary. It could only come to seem a feeble effort at self-justification. His portrait I paint with care from memory, with pity and nostalgia and without malice.

It was all evidence of juvenility, anyway, of arrested development. He was stuck at a stage every child goes through; just never quite got past it. All that whispering, for example. He had the habit, a habit he shared with his mother, of coming up very close and whispering, a habit as absurd as it was unsettling. What was all the whispering about? The old lady will do it still, as though someone might overhear her say, "Bring me tea," and there might be consequences. None of his whispered comments have stayed with me. It was trivia. But I think now, he had to know. He must have known that I, in all that winterizing, all that skirting, crawling around, was sure to come upon the evidence of his strangeness. He took so little effort to conceal it. Was he taking me into his confidence? What a profound disappointment I must have been. I cringe to think of it.

I recently looked again at some of the old photo albums in the living room of the big house. School portraits. The age progression. Such clear evidence in such a progression. Of regression. Mistrust and suspicion and a nasty, sneering, arrogant malice gradually creeping into his expression until it predominates, becomes fixed. Beyond a point, never again a relaxed, happy smile. Later still, never becoming a mature countenance, either proud, or concerned, or stressed and haggard even.

And then to watch him work—you never did see malice and resentment expressed so clearly, so thoroughly in the way someone worked: the way he turned a wrench, like he was tightening a garrote; the way he swung a hammer, like he was bashing in a skull; the way he stuck a shovel into the ground, like he was stabbing a pike through a prone adversary. He told me once about his method of getting to sleep: his sure-fire remedy for sleepless nights. In those restless hours, he related, he'd think up different methods, different schemes, to kill his parents. And get away with it. He didn't go into any of the gory details and I didn't ask, for example, if he'd come up with the perfect scheme. Or, coming up with it, if he'd put his plan into action. What am I saying? Of course, he wouldn't have. How could he have continued to torture them if they were dead?

More or less from the get-go, and for no good reason, I got into a somewhat unconventional sleep pattern: I'd fall sound asleep after scrounging the closest approximation to dinner I could find in my refrigerator. Just couldn't keep my eyes open after working outdoors in the wind all day and coming back to this cottage, which, then as now, I tended to keep a little too warm with the wood stove. Fall asleep at seven or eight, you're not likely to sleep right through till six the next morning. Often I'd find myself awake and fully rested at three a.m.

At that point I'd often have the feeling that I'd been woken up. I had the clear, distinct impression that someone or something was out there. So I'd step outside to the little stoop and, besides the wind, maybe hear the thump of hooves from a few deer trotting away. And so I'd shrug it off. Or try to. But that odd sensation of something out there wouldn't leave me alone. There was the wind; always the wind. You'll get sick of hearing about it. If you work outdoors here you get far more than sick of it. I always thought it an exaggeration to read about places where the wind drives people crazy.

Until I got here. You start to hear voices. Voices like a wild chorus of every vocal range, every age, whispering, speaking, crying out sometimes, all speaking at once, their own monologues in an exotic, guttural-sounding tongue, so that you seem to hear snatches, words, phrases maybe, that are vaguely familiar and seem to convey meaning with so much to choose from; bits and pieces of meaning among all that incomprehensible chatter. Then you stop yourself, realizing where this is leading. At best this is Hollywood B horror movie material. At worst it is madness. This is the work of dreams, with all this conscious hostility and strangeness in the air. This is what emerges from subconscious territory until it threatens to consume the conscious. Like the clear sensation of some—thing emerging from beneath these places. From beneath this place. You think this is what keeps me awake now night after night without even the evening sleep to compensate. No, this sensation has largely left. Flown the coop. I leave the superstitions to others and study the dream work for such insights as it yields.

Of all the unlikely meanings I've heard associated with the Indian name of our town, the only one I find has any resonance is *Restless Spirits*. Fits the place to a T. They spent a lot of time outdoors, it seems, listening to the same things I've been listening to. They did their burying out here. There are rumors of tunnels, vast prehistoric tunnels like the catacombs of Rome out in the hinterland between, roughly, here and the eastern tip of the island. I'll believe those voices in the wind constitute some vast telephonic network of souls before I believe in those tunnels. I've excavated these soils in dozens of, call them, test pits. Soils wholly unsuitable for tunneling; sands and silts and clays with plenty of rocks and boulders sprinkled in. Tunnels wouldn't last a decade in these soils, never mind five hundred or a thousand years. Wouldn't last long enough for the tunnelers to make it back out. But plenty of open land, and not so open—in fact, virtually impenetrable—enough to give rise to such rumors. Even if these soils were remotely suitable, tunnels presuppose a digging culture, a building culture, a tunneling culture and what evidence did they leave behind of anything like that? That this was the burial ground of the nearby mainland tribes came down through the oral tradition and made its way to the written records of the settlers, which suggests there's some truth to it. You think of the logistics of it, though, and it gives you pause: paddling across miles of open choppy water in a canoe, toting a corpse. Must have added plenty of spirits in the process. But how much of what was told the settlers by the local tribes can be believed, given that the latter were at the same time in the process of being eliminated by the former? Or those doing the telling, not knowing, may have made it all up. How many average people today have a clue about the burial practices of their own ancestors a couple of centuries ago? The local tribes taught the settlers to hunt mammals as big as houses from tiny open boats using spears and ropes. But they didn't write anything down. They had their priorities. So not much is known about the how and the where, although there's a plot of land with a plaque called Indian Burial Ground not far from here. Makes it all seem more familiar, I guess. Plenty of room for rumors, anyway, for speculation.

I'll take a stab at it. Here's my theory. Let's assume the burial crew in a canoe has made it to the beach with the corpse. I'd bring the corpse to a little rise not far from the beach. Somewhere with enormous boulders handy. Someplace with a good view of the sunrise. Or sunset. Take your pick; whichever seems the richer symbolism. Out here there are great views of both. You wouldn't want to do the digging between a rock and a hard place, or in this case, between two rocks. What you'd want is one hard place: a boulder so huge and deeply bedded it wouldn't be dislodged in the process. It provides the backdrop for the excavation; holds one side of it, so that the excavation is that much easier, doesn't have to be nearly as broad. Then whether the excavation is two feet deep or six is a matter of preference. Or, I suppose, of how often a trench is used. The boulder also doubles as a ready-made headstone. Then, maybe I'd leave the corpse in a crouch, facing the boulder, assuming the poor thing isn't already stiffened up in some other posture. More womb symbolism if you like. Actually, it also helps minimize the digging. Even assuming the corpse has already stiffened up in some entirely different posture, were these people—who could survive out of doors in this climate, who hunted whales from canoes—were they squeamish about modifying the shape of dead things? Would they have been put off by a little crunching? A little cracking? Then filling the hole back in would be a few minutes of work. Then on with the ceremony, the party, the ride back home. That's how I would have done it. Better yet, I'd get somebody else to do all the digging and filling in for me.

If I were an anthropologist or even a relic hunter, those boulders uphill from the beach are where I'd start looking. For evidence. Of course, I know, the shoreline shifts, recedes mostly. Call it one more attribute of the system; part of the beauty of it: after some time has passed, no more evidence.

Chapter Three

"What We Anticipate Seldom Occurs; What We Least Expect Generally Happens"

1.

*I*MAGINE THAT A NOVELIST would be sure to keep on throwing in all kinds of details about construction, so that you'd really feel his character's expertise. Unfortunately, I couldn't care less if you feel my expertise. Couldn't give the proverbial rat's ass; the proverbial *frijol*. I feel my expertise. Every time I move. I feel my expertise in my bones. On some level I can't help myself, as though I'm compelled, which is inexcusable given how little time I have left and that I might not have time to finish as it is. The nuts and bolts of our work are at best peripheral to the task at hand, the matter under consideration. The case before the court.

Frankly, reading about construction bores the living daylights out of me. Or take all these 'how to' videos and TV shows about building and renovation: you couldn't pay me to watch them. I understand why they're popular. People want to save money. They're sick of being held hostage by self-styled big-shot contractors. Who can blame them? But why would I want to inflict upon others that which I flee from myself? An aphorism: don't inflict upon others that which you flee from yourself. A fortune cookie. That's where the chapter titles come from: fortune cookies. Puppy Palace. With any luck I'll get to it.

I know you're not reading this for the fun of it, by the way. I know that. It's your job for some reason. Poor you. Hope you don't have to go out there and dig him up, too. Maybe you have good help. Some of what follows, I admit, I confess, I already had written out in some form or other and so merely have to clean it up and put it into some kind of order to stick it in here. Confession #4. Feel free to skip ahead, then, if what you're after are the facts, just the facts, if what you want is the dirt. How far? I don't know that yet myself. You might want to start up again when you start seeing Junior and Senior and the old lady poking back up in the text. That'll put you on more familiar ground. Familiar dirt.

Lately the world starts to dim and take on the aura of twilight. The senses play tricks. One comes to doubt their validity. Dreams come at odd hours, any hours—sleeping or awake—attain a vividness that can rival or surpass that of the world, this cloudy, foggy, dreamy world. It occurs to me that, as I sit here it's about a century since the publication of the first attempt at a major scientific treatise on dreams. Is anyone any closer to understanding the process of dream formation? What do I remember of the good doctor's conclusions? It's been a while. Wish fulfillment. Long-repressed desires somehow mixed and matched with fragments of memorable recent experiences. Fascinating stuff even when it seems a stretch. Even when it seems far more than a stretch.

For some reason, a dream recurs. Perhaps I'll include the entire transcript, tacked to the end. With the sonnets. Exhibit B. The recent experiences? On two job sites in succession I'd seen two crews of men working in a manner I'd never seen previously. In the one case, sheet rockers were *rocking* a ceiling, screwing up sheetrock to a ceiling while standing atop stacked five gallon buckets, propelling themselves with twisting swivels of the hips, somehow getting the bucket stack to move in the desired direction. Swiveling around rhythmically while driving in screws with periodic upward thrusts of the hand holding the screw gun.

In the second instance, a concrete crew was pouring a basement floor. The concrete was sent in via a chute through a window. It was winter time and they had no heat source down there other than their equipment: three gasoline-powered concrete finishers. Once the wet concrete was in place, they sealed themselves in, shut up all the windows and the door to retain this small amount of heat so that the concrete would set up enough to finish. The air in their enclosed space got increasingly acrid, increasingly foul, so foul that I couldn't stand to be in the same space with them for more than a minute. Still they insisted the door and windows remain closed. They were down there for hours, gas motors chugging along the whole time. Came up looking like fish-heads after a three-day binge.

Then a simple little conversation. More or less to pass the time one day, to see what he'd say, I asked Catocho if there were schools or training programs back in his homeland for the various jobs the migrant workers encounter on coming to America. He wasn't offended. He chuckled. I don't remember much about the conversation that followed. Probably there wasn't much of it. He was always more than a little shocked that I was interested in anything about him: his past, his life, his opinions, etc. The dream certainly occurred that week if not that night.

Such ordinary occurrences and then such a dream: a visit to a remote and impoverished country. A local guide, more voluble but otherwise bearing a remarkable resemblance to my quasi-legal tender. A dusty, desolate town in the midst of its annual festival, culminating in a series of contests, all held in the bullring at the edge of town. Each contest features ordinary tasks or jobs, carried to absurd extremes, so that by the end of each, only one contestant is left standing. The rest stagger off with assistance or are carried off. One champion is proclaimed for each contest. One contest after another, through a broiling hot, seemingly interminable day.

The second to last contest is held in the most intense late afternoon sun. The contest pits teams on rattling rotating contraptions belching thick black smoke that engulfs the entire ring and arena, leaving everyone and everything covered by a layer of the greasy exhaust and all but a few of the teams of contestants unconscious. The contestants with their whirling contraptions transform the ring from pitted and uneven sand and dirt to a brilliantly gleaming level pavement, the ideal surface for the final event.

The final contest is the race of the bucket dancers, which also leads to the culmination of the entire festival, held towards evening as the day yields to twilight. While standing on buckets, the contestants are to race around the perimeter of the bullring, now paved and polished to gleaming perfection. Each contestant begins atop a single bucket, swiveling rhythmically then thrusting up one arm after each three twisting movements. With each pass of the finish line a bucket is added to the contestants' stacks. Round and around the perimeter of the ring they go. The field shrinks as they topple off the increasing stacks of buckets until only one man is left. This triumphant dancer, perched on his impossible stack of buckets, continues his rotating, swiveling dance. He gradually turns inward until he's at the very center of the bullring, then turns round and round in place.

An enormous celebration ensues. Everyone pours out of the bleachers: the spectators, the former contestants of this and all the previous events, the attendants and officials. Bands strike up, enormous volumes of the locally distilled moonshine are drunk; everyone jostles good naturedly for a bucket. Those who somehow land two are quickly and playfully bounced off, the buckets redistributed. The joyous bucket dance celebration continues through the night.

Then the crowd slows its dance and those nearest him reach up to their champion, still dancing there at the center of it all. He holds out his arms and falls into their waiting arms. Now the dance becomes a procession. This huge throng gradually leaves the bullring and makes its way down the main street of the town, holding aloft their champion and the champions of all the previous contests, a garland of roses around each of their necks, each with a travelling bag in one hand. The music continues but slows, gradually, perceptibly, until it becomes the music of departure finally and then the music of final departure. At the edge of the town, the border of the desert wilderness to the north of the town, the champions are lowered to the ground. They are hugged, caressed, kissed; spoken to with the gentle tearful whispers of final farewell.

The light comes into the new day and I study the surroundings of the town, particularly the seemingly endless desert wilderness to the north. My guide appears, red-eyed and bleary from the aftereffects of the celebration in combination with all the tearful farewells. He informs me that these champions will now embark on their journey. Their destination is the Promised Land, a land of milk and honey where everything is possible and where everything works as it should. But first they must undertake this journey that brings with it certain challenges: the endless desert wilderness we saw before us, then an equally extensive mountain wilderness patrolled by large packs of voracious wolves, then a broad lawless borderland controlled by devils in human form, humans in name only for whom migrants such as these are prey and sustenance and nothing more. All before their arrival. To the Pearly Gates. To my question of when the voyagers will return he merely chuckles briefly and then changes the subject. Then he startles me by weeping while hugging me and thanking me for the privilege of being my guide to the festival and festivities. I am surrounded by the mournful crowd, each trying to hug me and caress me and thank me and offer words of encouragement. I turn, finally, from this appalling excess.

In the end I am in the wilderness, alone, holding a little travelling bag, a garland of roses around my neck. The crowd recedes towards the town. I start to return to them but my guide sees me. He stands now at the edge of the crowd, a whip in his hand; stands shoulder to shoulder with a formidable-looking group of men, their deadly glances directed at me. I turn back to the wilderness and begin to walk.

2.

Each time the dream recurs it yields more details but it always ends the same way. As I've mentioned, Catocho wasn't much of a conversationalist—perhaps the understatement of the new millennium—so when I filled him in about the dream of the bucket dancers, an even briefer summary than I've presented here, there wasn't much reaction. He told me about the festival in his home town. They had a Ferris wheel. Excellent *carne asada*. With regard to dreams, he was a literalist. A traditionalist. Certain things stood for certain other things. They told you about the future, not the past. The outside, not the inside.

Tell me your theory, about your research into dreams. I promise I'll listen. Not that we had much time, usually, to discuss dreams or much of anything else. It's just that there comes a time during the day, you're done running around, you're done using power tools that are rattling your brain and every nerve in your body, you're in a sweet location, there's a mockingbird up there going through its repertoire, a nice day, you're doing something that requires lots of skill and experience, but you've got both the skill and the experience so you can relax and proceed, just an hour or two left in the workday; next thing you know—voila—you have a thought. You want to share it with somebody. That's all I'm talking about. He was always more than a little appalled that I wanted his thoughts or opinions about anything; as though it wasn't his place to have opinions or at least to share them with me. Something like that.

It was clear, for example, that many of the events, much of the news of the day, was not much on his mind. Nobody had ever asked his opinion before on most of these topics. Perhaps not even himself. No one he'd worked for had ever wanted to find out about him either, about his life. Just the opposite: show me your papers. That'll do. Here's your shovel. Which was fine by him. He was here to work, not venture opinions. Not make trouble. On St. Pete's crew, there were a couple of other contractors who, like me, had the annoying habit of treating him like a human being. Since they'd be rattling on in English and his English was, to say the least, shaky, he'd give them the 'uh-huhs.' 'Uh-huh, uh-huh, uh-huh,' he'd say and I'd know it was all sailing right past him. He'd 'uh-huh'd' me often enough so that I knew enough to try to get the thought across in my equally shaky Spanish. His Spanish was shaky too, but that's a different story. Often as not, if I brought up some topic he hadn't heard much about or thought much about what I'd get in response was an echo. He'd just repeat what I'd just said, which, needless to say, got old fast.

He knew he was no fool—lord knows I knew it—and he obviously didn't consider the fact that he had only a second grade education much of an obstacle. He loved his work. He was good at it. He was acknowledged by one and all to be an exceptional worker. Even among his compatriots, the other quasi-legal and flat-out illegal and the other recent immigrants, he was recognized as an exceptionally good worker. Those were the opinions that mattered to him. And mine, regarding his work, an opinion that never varied or wavered. Still I'd try, you know, to talk about this or that. If I wanted him to respond, I had to hew pretty closely to his interests and experience. Of course, the fact that he was largely content with his own thoughts and completely focused on whatever he was doing was one of the good things about him. One of many. He was an easy man to be around. Quick to laugh. Self effacing. What's more, self-sufficient. Sure of himself. He knew his abilities; by and large he knew his limitations. At peace with himself; as I say, content with his own thoughts. Neither of us wanted a radio playing, for example. When we weren't running power tools, there were birds to listen to. Surf; wind. Thoughts. There was work to concentrate on.

Money. Money he could talk about. He was keenly interested in money and business. I had to be careful, raising the topic of money. It could cost me. I could usually tell when he was working up to asking for a raise: he'd start spinning the knob. The little knob on the hand crank of my truck windows could spin around. When we'd be driving around together, and he started spinning the knob, I knew he was on the verge of asking for a raise. He'd get fidgety. Uncommonly chatty. Whiny in a sort of sing-songy, ritualistic kind of way. This is a man who never whined or complained about anything. Give him a task that nine out of ten would run from, he tackled it with enthusiasm; with authority. This was different, like an exotic ritual you'd expect to come across on some South Pacific island. That was my take on it. Coming from a place where scarcity was the norm, this was how it was dealt with: you concentrated your whining into the short interval leading up to asking for a raise so that such thoughts and conversations didn't consume every waking minute. That's my theory, my hypothesis. As I say, he usually didn't whine about anything. He'd been through plenty: seen young siblings die, seen army buddies shot to pieces. Killed men, sometimes at close quarters. He was glad to be where he was, doing what he was doing.

Immigration and his own experience he could talk about, which I think is where the whole business about the dream of the bucket dancers comes from: an innocent attempt on my part to have a conversation. That'll teach me. His opinions on immigration could be surprising; surprisingly stern. Once during one of St. Pete's jobs off the island, we were all sitting around in the hotel room watching the news on TV before going out to dinner. A news story came on about a rally somewhere out west in support of illegal immigrants. "That would be a great time to grab them," he said. He said it to me alone, in Spanish, so he wasn't playing to his audience. He just didn't like the idea of people airing their grievances in the street. When something would come on about young Latino gang dudes, I could watch his blood start to boil. An army man. A law and order man. He had no use for troublemakers or attitude cases of any stripe. He'd have gladly joined the army in this country if they'd have let him.

He showed me a picture from his army days, some kind of large official document. I forget what. A large picture. He was standing next to his rifle, the rifle almost as tall as he was. Back then I would not have wanted to meet him in hostile circumstances, let's put it that way. Looked like he'd slit your throat in a heartbeat and then sit on your head while he calmly ate his rations. That's not quite right. It should be: looked 'as though' he'd slit your throat and then sit on your head while he calmly ate his rations. There, that's better. Fortunately, I met him in friendly circumstances every day. He was a sweetheart. No meanness in him. We hardly ever raised our voices with one another. Why would we? There was no need. I gave him his raises; never made him wait for his pay. His mistakes were all honest mistakes. Goofs. Usually trivial. Often my fault. He started anticipating;

knowing so well what I wanted done that he'd just go ahead and do it without my saying anything. Start before me. Since he got to the job site before I did, I wasn't always there to give him precise instructions. That sometimes got us into a little hot water. Didn't it, though? But now who's anticipating?

Sometimes the topics of money and immigration converged, as for example when he asked if I'd marry his wife. Don't ask me how this was supposed to come about or what it was to entail. I didn't ask. This was before I'd met Ellen, of course, and lord knows I've thrown it in her face often enough. (She fires back, "She can have you," without missing a beat, and then I am deeply hurt.) He offered to pay me five thousand dollars. I said to him, this is America. We don't do it like that—it'll cost you five million. I'd met his wife. Five million was a bargain. Anyway, I told him INS had a nose for fake marriages by now; it would never fly. I thanked him for the offer, though. It was kind of a gracious offer, come to think of it. It said a lot about him, I think; about us. I happen to know he didn't go around asking just anybody to marry his wife.

3.

St. Pete would do that routinely, by the way. No, not marry his quasi-legal tender's wife. Put us up at fancy hotels near his job sites off the island. That's just the way the man was; he couldn't help himself. Catocho and I often mused that we'd gladly just set up cots in the gutted house and split the hotel money, but that would never fly with St. Pete.

It seems so unlikely I can almost forget it was through Junior that I met St. Pete's construction manager during the summer of my first full year and so first came to work for St. Pete. To Junior, St. Pete was merely an Avis client. Didn't make the first tier and so never would. He wasn't old money. He'd actually worked in construction in his youth. Much later he started and ran one company; sold that. Started another. Built it into a world-wide operation; a powerhouse of zeroes and ones. All this counted against him in Junior's eyes. Golden Geese didn't work; they had little worker bees, drones. They condescended; they didn't respect. That, at least is my view of Junior's view. There's no other way to account for it. Junior was one of those contractors St. Pete tolerated around the margins; not part of his regular team. During his last six or eight years, Junior's primary occupation, other than torturing his old parents, was a painting and refinishing business known euphemistically as José B and C Painting and so, in this capacity he introduced me to St. Pete's main man and St. Pete, which led to one job after another for Catocho and me, ultimately evolving into virtually a full-time gig. This, by the way, was yet another example of how I owed everything to Junior, of how I was an ingrate and a betrayer. But why go there at the moment? He comes back into this soon enough. There's no getting away from him.

We'd set up a little shrine on each of St. Pete's job sites, a plaster or concrete garden statue that we invariably renamed Pete no matter which saint he was meant to resemble; set it up in a quiet corner of the job site, usually a much-frequented spot for lunch and breaks. We'd toss crumbs of sandwich bread or meat scraps or small coins at his feet, at his base, something the statue seemed to imply he was also doing. A regular contingent of birds, chipmunks and squirrels would come for the scraps, sometimes almost as soon as you'd toss them. The coins would remain a little longer though they'd eventually disappear as well.

St. Pete had an old carpenter on his crew, a man about ten years older than himself. This old salt and I often lamented that we'd met St. Pete so late in the game, as though we'd found ourselves unexpectedly in the clear near the mountaintop after a long slog up a muddy overused trail. He introduced me to the concept of a gam, which meant the considerable running of the gums that occurred between crews and between officers whenever two whaling ships came alongside. Whalers and fish-heads had nothing on him; he could unravel a yarn with the best of them. His family went back on the island to a couple of the original wanderers from the Pilgrims' colony. "Back then," he'd say, "they weren't afraid of a little dirt." He meant storms; rough seas; dirty weather. He knew about the old sailing ships and steamers, the whalers and the commercial fleet. He knew the currents, the winds, the reefs and sandbars and the individual infamous submerged rocks. He knew many of the wrecks from olden times, not just their names but exactly where they'd gone down and why and sometimes the names of some of the individuals who'd been on board. And what they'd been doing on board.

I had little to add. What did I know? I know

next to nothing about boats or the sea. I could listen. I only had one story suitable for a gam, that of the luckiest man in the world, which I can tell in abbreviated, regular or extra long, but how many times can you get away with telling the same story? I also know two jokes, the one about the brick kiln and one other. The one about the brick kiln is my idea of the perfect joke. Actually, it's more of a riddle. It cracks me up every time I think of it. But it's quite brief. By the way, that old carpenter didn't much mourn the passing of the old days. He knew the island had never been paradise on earth. You could tell by the way he talked about it that being a kid out here in the forties and fifties had been pretty great, but it was nothing he could ever hope to replicate for his grandkids. He also knew a number of the old families that had parlayed relatively modest real estate holdings into many generations' worth of college tuitions. His own family hadn't been so lucky, but he had the old house. A good boat. Life was good. He'd ride this one last wave with St. Pete; then call it a day. Sounded like a plan.

St. Pete's jobs weren't about sitting around spinning yarns. They were as taxing and demanding as any other, often more so. The work was what it was; that was how he'd put his team together in the first place, after all. We knew our work. Didn't need hand holding or baby-sitting. No shortcuts; only your best work; only your best thoughts. In return he gave you the sense of security that comes from knowing there's a sure hand at the helm. The work would be there; there'd be more. Lay out what you need to; the payment will be there before you need it, always more than fair; always generous. There were those who mistook his decency for weakness or stupidity. We ratted them out mercilessly and unrepentantly: the shortcut artists, the thieves, the milkmen. These were his family's homes: first his own family's summer home on the bay outside of Ponnack, then his sister's house (the man renovated his sister's house at his own expense as a gift), then a guest house—much smaller, but in a sweet location near one of the sheltered inlets. Later on there was a brick townhouse over on the mainland for visiting clients and other projects farther afield. Later still there would be investment properties and properties in which we, the builders, could invest. That was the theory and that's jumping pretty far ahead and anyway it never came to pass, at least not for us. His business was booming, and the man loved construction projects. He could turn to his construction projects in the manner of a challenging diversion as others might, say, competitive chess or bicycle racing. Took his mind off all those zeroes and ones, I guess, all those business loans and complicated deals. A diversion but not merely a diversion. When he was with us on the job sites, he was all there. He wasn't there for kicks, yucking it up. He seemed to like nothing better than to pull people together to look something over, to figure something out, to see the lights come on, to get it right not just overall but in all the particulars.

Abstractions. They illuminate neither the man nor the process. Guess you had to be there. Try to put goodness, rightness, down on paper; it slips away, slips through your hands, isn't quite believable, comes across looking pale and lame. Evil on the other hand is a snap. Evil is believable and memorable and suitable to any medium.

For Catocho, good and evil were no mere concepts, abstractions, metaphors. For Catocho good and evil were personal, present, very real. He loved St. Pete; would've gladly taken a bullet for him. The rest of us would have, too. Figuratively; metaphorically. He would have actually. Literally. For me, too. Yes, for me, too. Confession #— whatever. Catocho brought as much to the St. Pete's jobs as I did, an added benefit to me. No more scrambling to keep him busy. There was always something else going on where his help was appreciated. The man could pack a dumpster. The man could move materials; wield a sledge, a wrecking bar. The machine. My little red bull. Everyone liked him—he was hard not to like—and everyone loved his work, but even when I farmed him out, he never forgot who brought him to the dance.

Chapter Four

"Patience Will Be Rewarded at Long Last."

1.

T HERE WERE SEVERAL other regulars on St. Pete's team. The one I became closest to was a young man who called everyone buddy and so, needless to say, before long was called Buddy by everyone. He was a carpenter but with broad abilities. And very bright. I don't mean he was smart for a kid who bangs nails or that he was a fast learner. He was both. I mean smart as in, *could-be-anything-he-puts-his-mind-to* smart. He had taken some wrong turns. He was always shooting himself in the foot. His fists and his friends were always getting him into trouble. He was wonderfully devoted to his young family. Not yet twenty, he already had a wife and child and I was rooting for him; rooting for them. I was old enough to be his father, and there were times when I found myself in the role. There seemed to be a new drama, a new escapade, a new episode in his life every time you turned around. He was plenty scrappy and wasn't afraid of much. Combined with his intelligence, that could get a young man into a lot of trouble. If he could only get through the next few years, get away from ninety percent of his friends. If he'd only stop shooting himself in the foot.

He did that one day, literally: shot himself in the foot. With a nail gun. Almost crucified himself. Almost fused his toes. He was lucky. Bandages and antibiotics. A few days of limping around. Personally, I've never liked nail guns. Cordless screw guns, yes. Nail guns don't make enough noise for guys to realize how dangerous they are. Guys who get comfortable with a nail gun end up leaving their finger on or near the trigger. Then they get distracted, concentrating on something else. Next thing you know they've shot themselves in the foot or connected their little *huevecitos* to their left thigh. That's what was so strange about that time with Junior, with me. He was paying attention. He was as sober as he gets, as mature as he'll ever be. His first shot. A shot across the bow. Or maybe just an accident. We'll never know.

It was the year after the wedding, almost three years ago. We were on a little side job of his, building forms for a slab for a patio extension. As I just mentioned, I prefer cordless screw guns. Pull the screws afterwards, bang and scrape off the layer of concrete, store the boards under somebody's deck to use on the next job. I never could see tossing out perfectly good materials just because they were a little used. Anyway, in this case I was looking down, holding two boards together for him to shoot when I felt the business end of the nail gun against the back of my head. "Good thing my finger wasn't on the trigger," said Junior. I suppose it wouldn't have killed me. Lobotomized me a little. Or a lot. I was lucky. The times that might have killed me involved falls from high places. Another metaphor. Another cliché. Yes, I took a couple of spills, even before Junior got into the act, but I wasn't the luckiest man in the world. I know that because I've met the luckiest man in the world.

One winter about twenty years or so ago, Boss Haas and I had a lull between masterpieces. Each of us having some spending money and about a month of down time, he went off for an extended ski vacation with his future wife and I headed south *for to conoce* a part of the world that was new to me. I found myself in one of the family-run inns that are as attractive as they are ubiquitous in Latin America, doing little on this particular morning besides reading the paper, drinking coffee, and occasionally watching and contemplating the work of the crew that was repairing the roof. The inn was also the home of the family who owned and ran it, the rental rooms arranged around the courtyard. The home and all of the rooms were in the colonial style: a single story of whitewashed stuccoed masonry, clay roof tiles, gently pitched roofs sloping towards the courtyard and away from the house in each direction. The construction crew was also a family business, with an older and a younger brother and their teenage helper. The older brother was clearly in charge. He was cutting rafters from their work area on the ground. They were replacing some of the rafters—fairly heavy hardwood timbers spaced about three feet apart. Straps of lath were nailed perpendicular to the rafters to carry the roof tiles. The whole arrangement looked pretty light given the weight of the clay tiles, though they only used mortar on the lower couple of courses. Apparently gravity and inertia held the rest in place; they weren't fastened in any way.

The foreman was a striking-looking man: looked as though he'd stepped out of a Renaissance painting or perhaps had just painted one—a lion-like Mediterranean head, swept-back wavy hair, full but neat beard, not tall, but strong looking in the way of a man who gained his strength through his work. He had a very mature, calm, intelligent demeanor; very much in charge without being loud or bossy. He was cutting the rafters with an electric grinder rigged up with a circular saw blade. Of course it had no guard. The thing looked like trouble; looked like death. He would hold it as tightly as possible and ever so gently ease it down into the wood. Still it bound and pulled repeatedly. I wasn't watching him when the accident occurred. At that point his cutting table was set up just out of my view around a corner along the last corridor of rooms. He gave more of a stifled gasp than a shout, as though in experiencing a life-threatening injury, he also needed to remain cognizant of not disturbing the guests, then came into view and flopped down into the courtyard, curled up, a pool of blood spreading around him. At this point the Chinese fire drill went into high gear. A taxi was called to take him to the hospital. It occurred to me that he might bleed out before they got him there. I told their teenage helper to grab a towel and put pressure on the wound, which seemed to be in the upper thigh of one or both legs. The expression and gestures of this boy remain with me as clearly as on that day. *After you, sir. He's all yours. Be my guest.* The hand gesture; the expression. No words could have served as well. I picked the man up and pressed his legs together as he put his arm around my neck. He seemed as light as a child. Later it dawned on me that he was carrying much of his own weight by holding on to me like that. The taxi arrived. The hospital was nearby. The emergency room had a doctor and a nurse on duty and not much else going on. The doctor had a rather tired, bored demeanor. We see such things and much worse every day, his expression seemed to say. He stuck his finger in the dike. They showed me where to get cleaned up and the taxi took me back to the inn.

The next day I went to visit the patient. He was resting comfortably in a quiet, nearly empty ward off a leafy outdoor corridor. He had the preoccupied air of a man who's thinking about all the things he's not getting done, but he seemed genuinely pleased for the visit. The blade, he said, had come within a centimeter of severing the femoral artery. "Ah, what luck," I said. "Yes," was all he said, without emotion. Then he lowered the bed sheet to show me the wound: a nasty gash that crossed the upper part of both thighs, stitched together expertly with dozens of sutures. He was naked below his hospital gown and I couldn't help but notice what would have been severed clean off had he not been wearing rather tight-fitting briefs the previous day. I think I chuckled a little. "What luck," I said again. "Yes," he repeated, with the calm stoicism that entirely fitted the man. I didn't wish him luck as I left him. The man owned the franchise.

I know it's not much of a story. The sad part is, it's also my only story; the only one suitable for a gam, anyway. I was told that more than one carpenter had switched from boxers to briefs after hearing it. That's my justification for including it here, of course: as a public service. Thankfully, I've never come across a carpenter in this country who had to use a jury-rigged auto body grinder rigged up with a circular saw blade. Their work is hazardous enough here, lord knows, what with the tools they use, the places they work, the music they listen to. Nail guns, to me, seem to have a particularly sinister quality. Take most tools that can kill you: sawmills, chain saws, circular saws: when they're in that mode you know it. Their noise is already hurting you. Nail guns just lie there, coiled up, hissing at you. I've never liked them, not even before Junior took his shot; got into the act.

2.

We stored all kinds of things under people's decks; developed our own little network of under-deck storage facilities. Not bad stuff; not garbage, and nothing that was in the homeowner's way. In fact that was our prime criteria for a space to become part of our ad-hoc network: the homeowners had to *not* be using it. For any purpose whatsoever. Preferably they'd never so much as looked at it or considered it or knew it existed. The few times I bothered to ask them for permission they'd give me that look, as though to say, why bring up something so trivial? You develop a rapport, a sort of friendship. We did all sorts of things, all manner of chores related to their houses for regular clients in the off-season. What were a few bricks or form boards neatly stacked under their deck? That's all we're talking about here: odds and ends of construction materials left over at the end of a job, things I couldn't bring myself to throw out since they were essentially new: a few concrete blocks or a few dozen firebricks, plaster lath, lengths of flexible drainage pipe, odds and ends of lumber. Usually decks with only a foot or two of space under them. If they had more space the homeowners would invariably be using it themselves. We'd need some little tidbit on another job, and I'd say to Catocho, "Don't we already have that?" Then we'd both stand there star-gazing for a minute until one of us said, "Peabody's!" or "Tomasso's!" or "That place on Tidewater!" Often Catocho would get it before I did. He might have made a good game show contestant.

You might wonder why we didn't tote the stuff back here to the cottages. I asked the old lady about it. Around the cottages was off-limits. That was understandable. Skip would have to make a place in his yard. Junior's yard, his playpen, was a labyrinth, a forbidding, nasty place. I wanted to put a sign on his gate: "*Abandon hope—*" I went there often enough, to help him load or unload something or just to find him. He was a tinkerer, was Junior, and a pretty fair mechanic. The evidence, the wreckage, was all over his yard. I could never bring myself to ask him for a corner of it. Lord knows what it would have cost me. Didn't I already owe everything to him? Our under-deck storage system worked well enough, and the locations were often more convenient than coming all the way back here. It comes to mind lately in an entirely different context. Lots of stuff still under there. Stuff we never went back for. Nothing rotten. For the most part.

That aside for the moment—as though I could set it aside—a profound feeling settles in sometimes, particularly in the off season. It's as though things return to a primeval or at least pre-Columbian state, or at least want to, at least start trying to. It doesn't take long. You see all kinds of funny scenes: a family of ducks or geese walking down the sidewalk in one of the downtowns. Just last week I was driving past a row of shops near the docks towards evening, past the shops and stores and restaurants where last summer vacationing families and couples strolled along in leisurely fashion, a small herd of deer was calmly doing the same: strolling along a brick path, studying the store windows, I imagined, hunting for bargains. I wanted to tell them the off-season's when things are only twice as expensive as they should be. All the vacant houses—pranksters and vandals and thieves find the vacant houses irresistible and there's nothing particularly profound about that. It doesn't seem to be an enormous problem since everybody installs security systems. Still, things need doing. Storms need to be cleaned up after. People need to be let in and out. Every contractor seemed to have *his* houses. Junior, of course, had his tiered system. You find yourself there at somebody's house, at *your* house, you've done your good deed, it's lunchtime. Who could resist hanging out on the deck for a while on a warm autumn day for a meal and a gam; a little break? Who would mind? Again, I'm talking about clients with whom I was on the best of terms, not waltzing onto some stranger's deck.

Those moments are the origin of the thought mentioned above, about history and prehistory, and ownership, a thought that turns out not to be all that profound when you trot it out into the daylight and look it over: someday this all goes back, or sinks. Or the ice comes back to wipe the slate clean. "How did the deer get out here?" my daughter asked me recently. "Walked?" I speculated. "Walked? Across the water?" No, across the land, after the ice had left and the land had rebounded and before the seas rose a few hundred feet. I spared her some of the details, though it's amazing what she absorbs, what she asks. It's a guess anyway—the part about the deer. In the off-season, hanging out on somebody's deck, you get a feel for what it must have been like fifty years ago. And five hundred. As part of his ritualistic, sing-songy litany leading up to asking for a raise, one of the things Catocho would routinely say was, "How am I ever going to afford a house like this one?" Like the one we happened to be working on. And do you want the short answer? Or do you want me to spell it out in all its painful detail? Maybe there comes a time when the island's affordable again for any and all. Meanwhile save your pesos, amigo, for a home, a ranchito down in Catocholand. Which he did. As I say, in some perverse way this mess did work out. Not for everybody. No, not for everybody.

It was the origin of the under-deck storage system as well, the off season; that off-season feeling. That, "Who would care, anyway? Whose is it anyway?" feeling. They didn't care. They still don't.

Catocho began to intuit, to try to read my mind, as I've mentioned. His intuition wasn't flawless. Most often these led to trivial mistakes, goofs, things you could laugh about afterwards, as, for example, happened on a little side job of Junior's—almost all of our jobs for Junior were little side jobs, except the last, that fireplace. The job involved getting rid of some water-damaged furniture from one of the guest cottages of one of the Golden Geese. Some of it we salvaged; one desk Junior and I brought to the dumpster at St. Pete's job site. Then everybody went home. Except that this particular Goose called Junior. That desk was some kind of family heirloom. She wanted it back. Would I go get it? asked Junior. I would. Only I didn't. I was tired. It could wait until the morning. The desk wasn't in the dumpster. It was beside the dumpster. *Beside the dumpster* was Catocho's cue. Beside the dumpster meant 'dumpsterize.' The man could pack a dumpster. The man could wield a sledge. The man loved his work. By the time I got there to fetch it the next morning that desk was in pieces. Splinters. That desk was so neatly packed in the dumpster it would have been easier to retrieve the files from a computer that had been melted down into a lump of goo than to reconstruct that desk.

My fault, obviously. I certainly didn't blame Catocho. Everybody got over it. In fact, the thing was no heirloom; it was a moldy piece of plywood furniture that became an heirloom in Junior's eyes, in Junior's retelling. By then, only a couple of years ago, I already had three strikes against me in Junior's eyes so what did it matter? Catocho and I found the situation kind of funny from the get-go, I have to admit. I confess. Had the thing been worth anything he'd have saved it out for his own place. I only mention it here as an example of his interpretation of my wishes gone astray. By his second full year with me I often didn't have to tell him anything other than where the job was and what we were doing. The rest was a matter of a few brief comments. We never raised our voices with each other. Hardly ever. Why would we?

I think I've mentioned somewhere that Catocho had little patience for sitting around taking breaks. Wherever he is at the moment in Catocholand, I'll bet he isn't sitting around, and if he's happy, I know what he's doing: working very, very hard. When we started for St. Pete, he thought he had no choice in the matter. I'd say it was break time, and he'd follow me to wherever the cluster of break-takers happened to be. He'd watch me with anticipation for any signal that our break was over and be back at our work long before I'd get there. He just didn't like the concept of breaks so when it became clear to him that it was up to him, he simply stopped taking them. Twenty minutes, maybe a half hour for lunch, then, back at it. If he missed something good, I'd try to fill him in as we worked. On the townhouse job site on the mainland towards the end of a routine day, St. Pete's construction manager and I remarked to each other, loudly and in Catocho's presence that he was clearly slacking off, that he had stopped and eaten lunch that day. He waited until the end of the day, then cornered me, as furious as I'd ever seen him. Why had we said such a thing? He had the right to eat lunch. Everyone had the right to *lonchar*. It dawned on me that he was serious and he assumed that we had been. That particular brand of humor wasn't done in Catocholand, apparently, or, at least, not by him. On another occasion I repeated a particularly ugly bit of Spanish slang, not knowing exactly what it meant. Never in his life, he said, had he said those words. He wasn't kidding about that either.

He wanted instruction. Direction. *What do I do? What do I do now?* Not conversation. Not opinionating. Interpretation wasn't his strong suit either. Interpretation got him into trouble. Us, rather. Didn't it, though?

3.

Boss Haas, the Baass, found me out here not long after I arrived. We hadn't been in touch for a few years; then he sent me a little care package. It got to me after bouncing around northern New England for a while. Sent a couple of magazine articles in which he was featured. His latest awards and accomplishments. I wrote back. So they give out prizes now if you actually *can* think your way out of a paper bag? Or maybe for champion dumb-ass? He called. We laughed a lot. Talked about meeting up on the slopes somewhere. Or out here. He did make the trip to act as best man; spent a long weekend. It'll be four years in May. He didn't have much time and the rest of the family couldn't make it because the kids are teenagers now and didn't I know how that went? Yes, I guess I did. We'd get together again sometime. Only we didn't. We did find time to tour the island during that weekend. He asked about the island's history, historical patterns of development. Individual fine old buildings. Good questions. Sent me scrambling to the various libraries and museums once Ellen and I got back from our honeymoon week. I'd hoped to have him meet up with St. Pete since I was sure they'd hit it off. St. Pete needed a good architect. He'd have liked this good architect, I was sure of it. St. Pete couldn't make it to the wedding, and the Baass never made it back. Wouldn't it have been fun, though, to watch the sparks fly? That last stretch, those last few years with St. Pete, construction started to get meaningful again, or at least threatened to, at least had the potential to. It brought me back.

On our tour of the island that wedding weekend, the Baass and I would pause to consider each specimen of grand new construction. While I was prone to sweeping generalizations such as the old cliché, "Size is to home design as loud is to music," or "I'm waiting for some of these places to sprout gold-leafed onion domes," the Baass made no such sweeping pronouncements and certainly no sweeping condemnations. He's built some pretty grand stuff himself lately and how many architects can afford to poke fun at the design decisions of people who have tons of money to throw at their vacation homes? I knew he was no disciple of the 'bigger is better,' school of home design. Thoughtful, as always. Taking it all in. Studying the latest architectural clichés: the upward curving eaves, the eyebrow dormers, the second-story porches with cedar shingled parapet walls. All that exterior stonework. Different clichés from the ones he was used to seeing. 'Neo-traditional-beach-house-mansion': that was our oxymoronic label for the new stuff. They wanted to hearken back to the biggest and best of the early beach houses, the summer playgrounds of the families of the nineteenth and early twentieth century tycoons. Trouble is those places all had magnificent waterfront locations, so they looked like they belonged; whereas these places, as big and bigger in some cases, were plunked onto any old building lot that was left. Our shack in the White Mountains has a better building site than lots of them.

An interesting business: fittingness. Everybody has a sense of it. Like beauty. Time helps. The trees, the landscape grows up; the house settles in, acquires all those quirks and modifications that help give it character and personality. Humility helps, but it's not humility that I'm getting at. Or not just. Small can be plenty ugly. The Baass loved some of the neighborhoods of old fish-head cottages, by the way; there are a few of them left. I knew he would. Places where the boat in the yard's bigger than the house. Places shingled with fish-crates. Beautiful places, some of them, beautiful as yurts. A wonder that any of those neighborhoods have hung in there.

I could make a list of some of the details that routinely found their way into our little masterpieces way back when: there was lots of golden mean-ing, golden mean-ness; lots of openness—wide open spaces surrounded by wide open spaces; steep standing-seam roofs with skylights; timber-framing that allowed for all that openness; all that glass looking out onto superb western locations; massive stone fireplaces or masonry stoves; multiple gables and dormers; wrap-around porches; transformative restorations of settlers' cabins and farmhouses. I could go on and on with details and you'd start to get a sense of the palate he used, so much of which even then was in the process of becoming commonplace. You'd start to get a sense of the places, but it would never express what stopped people in their tracks. I showed him St. Pete's houses, the places we'd finished and the place we were working on. He got quiet, studious looking. I could see the smoke start to come out his ears. Really is a pity those two boys never got together.

We were bottom-feeders at first, the Baass and I, summers through high school and then college and then the first couple of years of really trying to make something of the collaboration. Who doesn't start out as a bottom-feeder? We took everything that came our way. It was all learning; it was all fun, even the little injuries somehow. Supermen back then. Wild men. How we laughed. Couldn't wait to get to the job site every day. Seems almost unbelievable to me now. Sliding down an unfinished roof, squealing like a stuck pig, then

Joseph M. Mascia

grabbing the last rung of the ladder that's hooked to the roof peak, grabbing it with one hand, then flopping around over the eaves like a fish being brought on board, still squealing, then pushing off and springing back onto the ladder, shouting calmly, "Never mind. I said, 'Never mind!'" Sweeping up all the roof crap: dried-up mortar turds and roofing crumbs and sawdust and plywood scraps and strips of lead—sweeping it all to the edge of the roof, then waving and blowing a big kiss down two stories before sending the whole mess down to infiltrate every shred of clothing and cling to sweaty skin for the rest of the day. Inventing reams of Esperanto. Diving off roofs into six-foot snow banks. Supermen. Wild men. All while doing cutting-edge work and helping to save—the universe. Not bad.

Superman no more. Zarathustra *sprachs no mas ad moi.* No more waking up and can't wait to get to the job site. The idea alone is pretty hysterical. And the ideas? They're all clichés now. Look towards the back of any rural-living-type magazine and see ads for houses much like we built. Only bigger. The McMansion version. That's the way it is in construction. How many brilliant ideas are there? Or even good ideas? You can't patent them, so they get copied. We realized that timber framing would allow for all kinds of openness, all kinds of possibilities that weren't practical with conventional framing. Lots of people realized the same thing more or less at the same time. Lots of homeowners liked the idea. Particularly young couples, it seemed; young families. Next thing you know you have the next bunch of architectural clichés. Our timber frame house plan ideas are modifications of designs we saw repeatedly in old barns, specifically New England barns. Originally? Got me. Wouldn't surprise me if some of these ideas evolved with the species.

Ideas in construction are a lot like musical ideas. Folk songs. There are only so many notes. Tunes follow from laws of tonality—patterns expressible mathematically, which, back in the day, even men of science assumed to be integral to the universal order. They might as well be. Stick to tonality and musical ideas, possibilities are drastically limited. Next thing you know you have musical clichés. Songs with different lyrics but the same tune. Or nearly so. Stretch the limits, start testing all the ideas and possibilities, and you start to lose the audience, which is fine, of course, as long as you don't need the audience. Stretch the limits too far, and you end up on the street, or they lock you up. Not always, though. Sometimes an idea catches on, eventually to become a cliché, or a marker of a particular era, a particular decade.

Or a material, a combination of materials comes along to open up new possibilities; reinforced concrete, for example. Concrete's been around for a long time, as I think I've mentioned. Maybe I haven't. I'll mention it now. Traditionally this was the alchemy that worked; the science of an unscientific age. It must have seemed pure magic: roast some powdered limestone, then mix it with sand and water at damn near any daytime temperature—a few days later it has strength and hardness approaching any rocks they were likely to find nearby. No wonder secret societies grew up around the craft. Not that they knew precisely what was going on in there; the hydration, the weak attractive forces, the precise chemicals involved in the precise reactions. They didn't have to. They still don't; don't know everything about it; the walls around the Institute for Concrete Analysis and Concrete Appreciation still somewhat mysterious to the scientists and engineers toiling within. Which calls to mind the one about the brick kiln: if bricks are made in kilns and kilns are made of bricks, where did they get the bricks to make the first kiln? I know, nobody gets it. At first. Just kills me, though, for some reason.

Some time, I think, mid-way through the nineteenth century, one man working more or less on his own in England studied the stuff—cement— refined the materials and standardized their preparation. The result is known as Portland cement, a product so ubiquitous it's usually just called cement. With Portland cement, concrete becomes stronger, predictable; you can pour it in the presence of salt water, and it still works. Add steel rods for flexibility, the next thing you know you have skyscrapers; bridges with extraordinary spans; the Hoover Dam; domes and cantilevering and curving structures such as could only be imagined previously. That's a pretty big deal since it changed the face of civilization in a big way. As to the other: individual construction ideas that catch on, how big a deal are they in the scheme of things? It's pretty mundane stuff when you get right down to it. We weren't discovering continents or curing diseases. We weren't even building things that hadn't been built before. But those moments, those moments when the lights come on. They don't translate, I suppose. Don't look like much in retrospect.

4.

We became connoisseurs of concrete, Catocho and I. We broke up a lot of it. And cut it and resurfaced it. Poured it, of course. That wasn't our specialty. That's just what we had to do to get to our specialty: all the hard stuff that goes over the concrete. Concrete still interests me, probably since it wasn't really what we did for a living. More of a sideshow. Remarkable stuff, concrete. I could go on and on about it. Concrete; mortars; cements. But I won't. We came to know concrete intimately, both in the placing and in the removal, the modification; maybe especially in the removal. I had—still do as a matter of fact—an array of drills and saws and small jackhammers. If the concrete had that light color, that almost chalky texture, which meant it was lean on cement and light on stone aggregate, it cut like butter and broke up in big, soft-edged chunks. Soft, pillowy concrete I called it. Nothing wrong with the stuff, usually, by the way. Whatever it had been doing it was probably working; just a softer, somewhat weaker version of the norm. Then there was the regular 3000 psi delivered stuff: plenty of aggregate, plenty of cement, not too wet when it went in. We found it everywhere: foundations and footings and all kinds of slabs. It broke up just fine and was easy to work: to cut, to drill, to chip off the surface for a better bond or just for resurfacing. Then there was the dreaded icy-blue pump-truck concrete. Cold-looking stuff. You knew it the minute you were into it. Smaller aggregate, but lots of it and a very high percentage of cement. It was fairly uniform so it flowed into place through a hose, so it made life easier for the guys who placed it, then it killed you if you had to break it up and take it back out. Your estimate was blown. If the job was for St. Pete, that's when you left an extra offering at the shrine. He understood.

Most often we mixed on site. Mixing was about the biggest part of Catocho's job. He loved mixing; concrete especially, I think. It met all his criteria. It was exhausting, heavy, dirty. I was going to say noisy, but he didn't really like noisy. Nor was mixing particularly noisy. Not compared to jackhammering or cutting with a wetsaw. Working together, using only my little electric mixer, we could mix and place five or six yards of concrete in a day, a day that usually included other tasks as well. That's nothing exceptional. It was a relaxed way to pour concrete, compared with calling for a truck, which was why I often preferred to do it that way. A day like that could be exhausting for me, particularly in the last few years. Not him. A day of mixing concrete couldn't be long enough for him.

If he was mixing mortar and setting me up with materials, whether he considered the job good or not depended on the materials. Block work was good. Blocks were heavy, both individually and together in a wheelbarrow. They had to be brought from wherever the cube was left by the truck to wherever I was working. If I was working from scaffolding or on a roof, better yet. The blocks had to be carried up to me. Towards the end, when my hands and arms no longer functioned very well, he had to help lift the blocks into place. Life was very very good. Brick jobs were okay. Bricks are light individually but put eight or nine of them together in a brick tong, they're heavy enough. They were heavy in a wheelbarrow. There was all the mixing. Stone work: not so good. Too slow. Veneer jobs involved, for him, lots of cutting, on the wet saw or a circular saw. Cutting was okay. Too noisy and not very heavy. Stones had to be brought and laid out, but progress was just too slow. There was some mixing at least. Some walls involved no mixing at all. Nothing but laying out stones for me. Then what? Selecting and placing stones was never going to be his work, and I rarely needed help lifting stones into place. For jobs like that he needed a side job nearby, preferably something involving lots of hand digging.

As far as he was concerned, hand digging was the best work of all. The man was a virtuoso with a shovel. I was second fiddle; second shovel. Not that I didn't do my share. Just that when it came to hand digging, he was the undisputed maestro. He dug as if his life depended on it. The best jobs for hand digging were foundation repairs and foundation waterproofing in locations where it was too tight for a machine. Not that it would have mattered to him. I could have pointed to an empty field and told him we were excavating for a house foundation. His only question would have been where to pile the dirt. I would never do that, of course, burn him out. For no good reason. Even if I needed to make work for him.

He could always sense when I was making work for him. He didn't like it. Make work was down time and, as I've said, he wanted no down time. Down time included days off, with or without pay (because if you gave him a day off with pay, which I did a number of times a year, he wanted to work anyway and so, double his pay.) Down time included time watching me work. Didn't matter if I was building something kind of tricky like a fancy firebox or a sweeping stone entry column. If he was watching me work, it was down time, and he didn't like it. If I gave him a job and said, "That's your job for the afternoon. Take all afternoon," he'd finish in a half hour and then say, "What do I do now?" I had to get sneaky: had to find things he could do but took him a long time. Stuccoing a block wall was the thing. He got good at applying layer after layer of gluey mortar to a block wall and buffing it smooth with a sponge, but it took him a long time. He didn't know that a lot of those walls didn't need any parging. He still doesn't. Why would you give a smooth, finished surface to a wall that's going to get veneered with something else? You wouldn't. But he did. Lots of times. He never knew. His understanding of the craft wasn't that subtle. Nor did I ever tell him. Suppose I'd say, just go stucco that wall because it'll get you out of my hair for a few hours? Better he didn't know.

We approached our ideal if I had something difficult and tricky going on that needed tending once in a while and he had a big hole to dig nearby. That was as good as it gets. That was as good as it got in the business sense as well, by the way, since I could then charge dearly for both of us. I suppose I should feel guilty about that, but, in fact, there's nothing to feel guilty about. Nothing cynical about it.

Take foundation waterproofing. I could paraphrase Mr. Youngman's joke because that's exactly how I felt about those jobs. They could have them. Still these jobs found me—us—repeatedly. Became something of a sideline specialty. Some nor'easter gale, some pile of dirt, would blow the daylights out of the island for three days and people would call because there was a gallon of water in the basement. Anywhere I'd worked before that was known as a dry basement. I've seen places where the water well is in the basement: kill two birds with one stone—might as well. I've seen streams running through basements. Now a gallon of water in the basement after a nor'easter could be a problem because there was hardwood cabinetry and designer furniture and electronic gadgetry with miles of wiring down there. I'd tell the homeowner exactly how we'd do it, too, as though to say, please hire somebody else; do it yourselves. I'd have set them up with the materials and the tools if they wanted. Still we'd get the jobs. It wasn't long before Catocho could handle the whole thing. It was all within his skill set, his comfort zone. He loved those jobs. We'd dig down to the base of the foundation; the base of the footing, wherever the water was getting through, and then away from the foundation far enough from the house to diminish the likelihood of burying ourselves; sometimes brace up all that earth, clean the wall up, usually just with a little water and stiff brushes, look for the tiny cracks, the fissures—there didn't have to be any—then parge on a couple of layers of the gluey waterproofing mud they talked me into using at my supply yard, then once things had set up, tar the daylights out of our new work, fill it all back in and get the hell out of there. I never liked those jobs—the prospect of burying ourselves, the lack of skill involved—despite the fact that they could be relatively lucrative. Catocho loved them. They were right up his alley.

I asked him about it: about how you get to be a virtuoso with a shovel, aside from the obvious, aside from out there in the corn and bean fields from the age of five; and the army, of course, the trenches. They dug a septic system once, down in Catocholand. He and one other man. For a hospital. They had a rope and pulley to hoist out the buckets of dirt. Removed a great cube of earth more than twenty feet on a side and more than twenty feet deep. They unearthed a boulder part way down. Having no way to hoist it out they let it follow them down; managed to do so without the thing squashing them like grapes. Dug a pit for it at the bottom and rolled it in; buried it. What were my jobs in comparison?

It's obviously a self-indulgence to go on about peripheral matters when I run a real risk of running out of time. The reader grows impatient; grows weary of digressions. Reader. Singular. One more digression—but it will need its own section.

There's also one of Buddy's escapades, one of the adventures of Buddy, that I should include—just a brief description. He told us about it towards the end of our time with the St. Pete team, not much more than a year ago, and since he generally told us about these things more or less as they were happening, in real time, as though he were both perpetrator and reporter, I think we can assume that it was all transpiring right about then as well. It seems there was an older member of Bud's extended family or a friend of a relative or a relative of a friend—who can keep that stuff straight? An old man to him, a man in his fifties, to whom Bud felt particularly attached, having helped him out repeatedly, taught him, given him tools. Now this old man, this crock, this relic from prehistory, was in poor health and financial need because he could no longer work, so he took on boarders, one of whom turned out to be a crack dealer and thief who robbed him and threatened him and was doing his best to terrorize him out of as much property as he could manage. So Buddy found this ambitious young fellow and first blinded him with Mace and then beat him senseless. I remember the Mace part making me uncomfortable, but I was rooting for Buddy and I was inclined to take his side. It's Catocho's reaction that I think about now, how when I explained that, in Buddy's eyes at least, this punk had given up even the right to a fair fight, just had to be left in no condition to continue doing what he'd been doing, that Catocho seemed to be studying me, as though for instructions. It didn't register much at the time. It just comes back to me now, for some reason.

Chapter Five

"Your Dreams Hold the Key to Your Future."

1.

WHAT *NOVELIST WOULD* continue to intrude on his narrative? For another description of a dream? I forge ahead, oblivious, following some murky compulsion. It's occurred in several variants and on several occasions, this dream, most recently not long before I started writing this. Once again the full transcript will be found with the sonnets. Exhibit C.

An evening gathering at which I'm to be the featured speaker. An informal affair, perhaps thirty or forty people. I learn my topic as I enter the room. I see it posted: *The Eureka Moment and How to Build Almost Anything*. Ridiculous. Absurd. These are two distinct if tenuously related topics, neither of which is suitable for a light evening talk. The former, the eureka moment, is a subject fit for a tome, a tome such as I use on sleepless nights—to cure them; a tome that will inform and instruct on many topics—other than the eureka moment, about which next to nothing will be imparted since next to nothing is known. Then, *How to Build Almost Anything*: truly a topic suitable for almost any medium—except a light evening talk.

Well, never mind, they only want to get through my part of it and then on to the eating and drinking, the cocktails and prime rib or whatever was being served. I'll open with a joke, tell a few stories, maybe get in the abbreviated version of *The Luckiest Man in the World*. You know, keep it light. And short. How far wrong can I go? But I get off on the wrong foot. I tell my other joke, an 'ugly baby' joke, the one where the doctor slaps the baby's mother. It falls completely flat. Not even a chuckle or a nervous twitter. For the eureka moment part I decide to talk about the chicken coop I tore down and rebuilt in my home town in Montana when I was just starting out, a structure that its owners wanted rebuilt for other uses. The project had a couple of good eureka moments embedded in it, I thought. Unfortunately I immediately veered off and started in about the young man who had helped me on the project, about his fondness for travel and his interesting habit of venturing out on meandering road trips that he funded by modifying scratch tickets, turning losing tickets into winners using nothing but warm water, surgical scissors, and corn syrup. After going on at some length about his exploits and adventures, including the inevitable humiliations and incarcerations, the verbal transition back to the chicken coop project was less than seamless. This young man managed to work with me for the entire three-week duration of the project without wandering off and getting arrested. Perhaps his parents cried for joy at this turn of events but my audience on this night was less than bowled over.

On to eureka moments. After tearing down the old chicken coop and beginning to reframe the new structure we decided it didn't look right. Something was wrong with it. Then we saw it. It was so obvious: the old coop had a low wall that corresponded to the side where all the chickens had lived, where all the cages had been built, but that low wall made no sense for the new users of the building, none of whom were chickens. We'd raise that wall, to match the other interior wall. But this created another challenge, since for various reasons the roof couldn't be raised, it would have to be shallower and this would make it weaker, more prone to sag or collapse under heavy snow loads. We decided to span the width of the building with collar ties now that the walls were high enough to allow it. The whole thing would be stronger, more tied together, better able to withstand the snow loads of the northern Rockies. And it looked right, too.

Well now, let's see. Apparently it hadn't dawned on me that I'd just detailed the most lame, insipid eureka moments in the history of light evening talks if not in history. The building is no longer for chickens. Make the low wall higher to accommodate people. Eureka? The roof pitch will then be shallower, so tie the rafters together with collar ties. Eureka? Having begun by squandering the audience's sympathy I had proceeded to fritter away any lingering interest. They sensed a swindle. Where they had hoped to gain insights into the inner workings, the mechanics, the nuts and bolts of the human mind, instead they were sitting through a long-winded, digressive story about a chicken coop. Some of them now had hostile looks and clearly wanted me to squirm and here I was, starting to comply. I was still standing there in front of them. My talk was only half over. There was still 'how to build almost anything.' I decided to change tactics.

How to Build Almost Anything. How boring. How trite. If you're building something and you need to find out how to do it, look it up. Let's talk about how—not—to build things. That'll be more fun. I recognized audience members. I singled them out for skewering. There was the couple with the oceanfront mansion who'd hired a crew of carpenters to build a rain forest's worth of mahogany-decked walkways through their perennial gardens, watched them bring the project to completion, including plugs matching the grain of the decking, including the varnish, then told them to tear it all out and start over. The walkways were a few inches too high off the ground. Tearing it all out meant chain saws and dumpsters; there was no getting at the screws. They were under the plugs. The plugs whose grain matched the grain of the decking. There was the couple who no longer did much in the way of communication though they managed to maintain a joint residence. They never used this home at the same time; still they contracted for extensive renovations, including a second floor master bedroom stone veneer fireplace. The husband would come to the house and instruct the masons to build the fireplace on one side of the bedroom and then he would leave. Weeks or months later, the wife would arrive, put a halt to the work and insist that the fireplace be built on the opposite wall. Then, weeks or months after that, the husband would come back and instruct the masons to stop, tear out their work and put the fireplace back where he wanted it. Back and forth the fireplace went, each time an undertaking so massive it involved tearing the house apart, rerouting plumbing, drainpipes, wiring, ductwork, finish carpentry, roofing, not to mention everything to do with the fireplace and chimney. I detailed all of this construction and reconstruction at exhaustive length, then painted a verbal picture of that fireplace being built and torn down and rebuilt endlessly, with never so much as a single fire kindled. Was it standing there finally, that hapless fireplace? And on which wall? And was the crew of masons, brought in from so far off on the mainland, finally freed from this Sisyphean sentence? In the audience was a different crew: chimney butchers, short-cut artists. I knew their work—I'd torn down so much of it. Here they were trying to egg me on, but I was having none of it. I lit into them. There was the architect and the builder who'd been responsible for the construction of so many of the worthless and dangerous chimneys and fireplaces I'd been called in to try to fix or replace by vexed and exasperated homeowners. There was the building inspector who turned his back while all of this was going on but found time to visit sites repeatedly to measure the depth of deck footings. There was—

2.

The woman who'd introduced me approached with a fixed, terrified grin. She hustled me off. "Let me give you a tour of the—facility," she said, and brought me down to the basement, which was full of junk. In a far corner of the basement she paused in her tour to show me the old wine cellar, a carryover from Prohibition days. From the outside the door to the room was barely discernible. There was, however, a wall switch—the old push button kind that she pushed to turn on the single bulb, which now glowed from the center of the ceiling of the little room. I followed the wires—separate wires exposed on the ceiling. Ancient wires with elaborate insulating brackets to keep the wires apart and in place. She commented on my interest in the wiring.

"Knob and tube," I offered. "About the most antique of residential wiring." She was smiling broadly and nodded encouragement, holding out her hand, inviting me to enter and examine the room. An intriguing little room, I had to admit—about ten feet on a side, all surfaces of concrete, including the ceiling. Rusted reinforcing steel was visible at the bottom of the ceiling slab; ancient whitewash peeling from the walls. The room smelled musty and dank and there was nothing much in it other than some piles of old newspapers and magazines, stacked on the floor. My tour guide was explaining about the windows. There were two windows, one cut into each of the side walls—small windows with wells outside several feet deep. She said these had been used for the booze boxes; the size of the wells and windows corresponded precisely to the size of the boxes the bootleggers had used. She encouraged me to look at the windows more closely but I needed no encouragement. I was studying one of the windows: the rotting wooden frame, the rusty metal grate that filled the opening, the smell of decaying leaves from the well outside. I was speculating to myself that only a small child could fit through the opening. Just as this thought occurred to me the door behind me slammed shut and a very secure-sounding lock was turned.

Having their little joke. Preparing a surprise, perhaps? What was the occasion? Would I be called upon to make another speech? Should I begin preparing some light, witty remarks? About what I'd found in the old wine cellar? And why had I been interrupted in my historical research? There was no wine or booze in the room, however. Only the old magazines and newspapers and those not in particularly good condition. The bottom ones were all but ruined by the damp floor. They were nothing special: no kind of collection, just old magazines dumped there waiting for someone to sort through them or, by now, more likely, cart them off to the dump. To give myself something to do while they prepared their surprise, I started to look through them, though I kept looking towards the door. The joke was getting old. I was also plenty hungry and looking forward to a relaxing drink or two after the stress of the evening talk. I was starting to become irritated, then heard footsteps outside the room. Finally! All would be forgiven, particularly if the surprise was good enough. I recognized the sound of the steps of the woman who'd given me my tour. "Knob and tube," she said through the door with her characteristic and annoying little giggle as she flipped the light switch, leaving me in the dark. The footsteps receded. I was too stunned to call out or say anything or even to move. What kind of joke was this? A bad one. Someone would answer for it. But how long would it go on? I felt for the door but there was no handle or latch of any kind on my side. I could barely distinguish the door from the surrounding wall.

No one returned again that night. I was forced to make an uncomfortable bed of old newspapers and crumple up a few for a crackly, smelly pillow. The mold and dampness left me stuffed up by morning. I'd slept badly and had only fallen soundly asleep shortly before dawn. Yes, there was mold; I had passed an uncomfortable night—someone would pay for this. This was decidedly not funny. This was decidedly—not—the way to treat the featured speaker for the evening program. The thought momentarily amused me. I'd use it down the line somehow. In a talk.

Footsteps outside the door woke me in the early morning. It was still pitch dark outside, which I sensed through those vent windows. Robins were chattering away out there. The footsteps, the shoes, were the same as the night before; the same silly, girlish giggle as she passed something through the small sliding panel in the door, which, by the smell, I sensed, was breakfast. The light snapped on. On the tray was some kind of hot cereal such as I never eat, weak coffee, fake cream in one of those little plastic containers. Cheap OJ in a small plastic cup. Cafeteria food; institution food.

I passed the day looking through and then sorting the publications in the piles in the far corner: these moldy and damaged beyond repair—rubbish; these not too damaged but not worth keeping; these few retaining enough interest for some historical reason; these with articles I wanted to read then and there. I made a little pile of these by my bed but didn't pause in my sorting. At the end of the day the sorted piles were removed, new unsorted piles left. The day turned to weeks.

One morning several weeks into my stay, at least several weeks, there were no more piles of newspapers and magazines to sort. Out in one of the wells was a single five-gallon plastic bucket, clean and empty but not new. And a short handle spade shovel. My breakfast that morning was much more hearty and substantial than I'd grown accustomed to. Inside the room, with the light on and daylight streaming in through the window wells I saw for the first time that there was a gap, a break in the outside wall, the wall facing the door, a surprising thing to have overlooked. Most of what I'd taken to be a concrete wall was nothing more than an earthen bank, sheer and even, but consisting of firm clay-like earth. I sensed as well that someone was outside, attached, as it were, to that shovel and bucket, waiting or anticipating, perhaps with some impatience. I brought the shovel and bucket into the room, the bucket barely fitting through the opening. Tentatively I started to dig.

It wasn't bad digging: neither hardpan clay nor soft sandy loam. I filled a bucket and maneuvered it back into the window well. Immediately a hand wearing a work glove grabbed the handle and took it away and brought it back empty shortly thereafter. One bucket after another I passed outside, always followed immediately, almost impatiently by its return to the window well. I probed the wall with the shovel, checking for the edges, checking for where the concrete ended and the earth bank began. Where I found earth, I dug. At midday my giggling jailer brought a much better lunch than usual. Again I sensed a certain impatience outside that window well as I finished my meal, hoping for at least a little break—it had been a while since I'd put in such a day of manual labor. Soon enough we were back at it. By the end of the day I could look at the earthen bank with a sense of accomplishment. At least I'd made a dent in it. By now it was clear that the side walls made the turn—they had corners, but there was an enormous break in the middle. Plenty of earth to remove out there.

3.

Day after day the excavation continued. More buckets appeared so there would be no lag time between passing up full buckets and getting back empty ones. Occasionally, there were stones to pass out; nothing enormous; no boulders. By the third day I was beyond the confines of the little room in which I'd started. There was still a solid roof over my head. Apparently that ragged concrete slab continued out past the dimensions of the room. The empty buckets were no longer placed out in the window well. Somehow they were simply tossed into the room. Later I no longer had to carry the full buckets out and place them outside the window. I merely had to set them up in a row back in the room. They were immediately taken away, the empties tossed back in. At some point I didn't even have to do that—just set the full buckets behind me where I dug; empty ones tossed back to me. Every time I paused for any reason whatsoever, I sensed the impatience of whoever it was who was helping me. There was no getting ahead of him. He was a slave driver.

The light from the little room grew ever dimmer. Then I left it behind altogether. The excavation had become a tunnel and while, initially, it was roomy and sufficiently lit, as I continued to move forward, passing full buckets behind me and having empty ones placed within my reach, the excavation closed in around me until I sensed damp earth around and within reach on all sides. Still, I was comfortable; my needs were being met. Even the darkness, the cool, damp earth was comforting, pleasant. I decided to rest.

No sooner had I settled myself comfortably into the soft moist soil and made a little pile for a pillow and rested my cheek against it and started to drift off than a mechanical noise from the far distance behind me startled me awake. I recognized the noise of the machine: a dirt conveyor such as we had occasionally used to help remove earth from interior excavations, from the basement of houses. I could hear the rhythmic slapping of a broken band, one of the rubber scoops that carried the dirt along the conveyor. Yes, it sounded like the very same machine we used to use. I waited with anticipation since the thing wasn't just coming towards me but must be coming for me. I sat up, as I did so scraping the top of my head against the ceiling of the excavation so that dirt was loosened and tumbled down my neck and back.

Not very far off, the electric motor of the dirt conveyor was turned off, and with it ceased the annoying *thwack, thwack, thwack* of the broken band. Soon another electric motor took its place, this one running a very quiet electric vehicle that approached very near and then was turned off. A beam of light came from this vehicle and as its occupant slid out of its seat and came up to me, he was surrounded by a ring of light, as though he'd brought the sun with him. The brilliant, magnificent light from his helmet shined into my much narrower compartment. When his light fell upon me directly, it blinded me. I sensed a benevolent presence. Was it St. Pete? I wasn't sure. Even after he dimmed his headlamp and set up another lamp on its own stand off to the side, a lamp that illuminated the space to perfection, I still couldn't see his face clearly. He considered my surroundings and then seemed to be studying me personally. He had a slight, warm, kindly smile. He settled himself into a comfortable seated position with his legs up, holding his knees. He seemed to be at some distance from me, though how much distance was there in this little space?

He very calmly and straightforwardly presented his offer: He was offering me a higher wage than I'd ever earned. I could take more time off, much of it with pay. I could start again immediately. I could go back with him now in his own cart. Just the way I was then. What was my answer?

I stared at him in disbelief. I started to shiver uncontrollably. What was my answer? Was he joking? Did he really think I'd leave all this? Did he have any idea, any concept of how hard I'd worked to create all this? And what it all meant to me?

He stared at me without speaking. I had no more to say and neither did he. He seemed to ponder the matter for a considerable length of time, then nodded finally, reached out his hand once more, turned out the lamp that had illuminated the space so optimally and withdrew. I heard the whir of his cart as it withdrew and then the *thwack, thwack, thwack* of the earth moving rig, also withdrawing, and then it too was silent. I was left in utter darkness.

Utter darkness and silence. No more buckets, full or empty, or shovels, or assistance, or anything. To continue now I had only my hands to scratch at the soil, pulling it from in front of me and drawing it to my sides and then kicking it behind me in a kind of swimming motion. This soon left me surrounded and in close contact with the cool, soft dirt on all sides. This movement of arms and legs, too, soon became impossible. Thereafter my arms remained close by my sides until I had no more sensation of arms or legs. I could only wriggle in a directional manner, guided by some unknown sense. Nor did it concern me. All notions of concern slipped away as did past and history and thought of any kind. Sensation alone remained of the fragrant, flavorful earth all around and of its passing in and through me. Sensation, movement—slow, fast, or otherwise; one way or another—directionality—this alone remained of thought, though it was or became entirely unconscious. Then movement, too, ceased, but not sensation. There was only this last sensation of rightness about this final location. How long I remained in this place, this state, was a concept, a notion as foreign to me as any other; time and duration had left me. It might have been a second, a minute, or seventeen years. What triggered or brought about a change to this state is also unknown. Movement, wriggling movement, at some point began again. And then the yes-ness and no-ness of directionality. Good and bad, right and wrong—this is all they consisted of. When movement became again the swimming action of arms and legs, it was as unconscious in its appearance as had been its disappearance. Then movement again had a goal: towards lesser resistance, towards the light. I sensed up and down and up was the direction that meant good. That meant life. It became imperative. It became a struggle.

I had to reach the light and reach it soon. This strangling earth with its tiny pockets of air to somehow be sifted through mouth and lungs—it wasn't nearly enough. I had so little time. But I had strength. I was nothing but will and strength. I must survive. I must get out. There was daylight, true daylight above me. It was almost within reach. I thrust great armloads of dirt behind and kicked it back, then grabbed another; one after another. Now

I had the sense of suffocation and near panic. Terror, too, returned and consciousness and all that went with it. One hand and then the other reached for and then reached the air and the light. Huge gulps of air entered me, and there was an indescribable sense of exhilaration. Life. It was so delicious. The joy of it was almost enough to choke me.

A hand reached and grabbed my own, helping to pull me up. Strong and firm. Familiar. Smaller than my own, and darker. Like iron that arm, that hand, that grip. I tried to clear my eyes. I longed to talk to, to hug this somehow familiar helper. He held firmly onto my hand with a hand that had, on its wrist a sort of heavy silver bracelet.

And with his other hand he slipped the other half of this heavy bracelet over my own wrist and latched it shut.

Chapter Six

"At the Touch of Love Everyone Becomes a Poet."

1.

I FIRST HAD AN INKLING that things weren't quite right with old Harold that first autumn here when I saw him using Junior's backhoe to dig up a shad bush out in a corner of the property. Transplanting time. He was working the controls pretty well, in the manner of someone who's comfortable on a piece of machinery but uses it only rarely: a little jerky with the hoe. He was doing okay, though. The trouble was he wasn't wearing a stitch of clothing. He obviously didn't consider this a problem, by the way. He was clearly as happy as the proverbial clam at high tide. When I showed up, the old lady was there beside the machine, shouting, pleading. He just kept on digging. When he'd heard enough of her, he tried to fling a hoe full of dirt in her direction. She bustled off to the main house.

It was a fairly warm day. A little breezy. Too chilly to be on a backhoe naked. I tried something that works with nine out of ten people, nine out of ten times: told him he had a phone call. Pointed to the big house. He idled it down and I escorted him. I wanted to hear if he had anything in particular on his mind. He didn't really. Just a nice autumn day. Good day for a little transplanting; a little backhoe work. Naked. Who could argue? His frame looked a little wasted, but he still looked strong. He was still taller than me by a good four inches; still had that full head of wavy white hair, that crooked little moustache. I had to hand it to him. He still looked as though he could swim the harbor pond, and then rescue a damsel in distress.

The next year the civil war took on a whole new dimension. Entered a whole new phase. Old Harold had had a bout of the flu that winter that had evolved into pneumonia, which he had barely survived. Now he was better, if you could call it that. Now he had decided to *let 'er rip*. Not that there was much of a decision involved on his part. The decision, I suspect, was largely out of his hands. If in some way he had chosen to spend his remaining time in a land of fantasy and delirium, who could blame him? What he was going through obviously wasn't much fun. It wasn't Alzheimer's; it wasn't Parkinson's. What was it? He was failing slowly. Who acts his best while his health is failing? He didn't wander off or forget who he was or who anyone else was. He lost all self-control, all inhibitions. He went all loopy. I know what you're thinking: where did I suddenly get the credentials to hand down clinical diagnoses like *all loopy*?

Sometimes it's hard to be humble. Some of what old Harold was going through was just ninety-whatever. The man was entitled. Even before then, as I've mentioned, he could be an ornery old cuss. I had always liked the old boy. The incident with the backhoe was just the mildest of the evidence of his condition. He turned wild; violent. Stopped sleeping. Then when he'd sleep, he'd crash so hard, sleep so long and profoundly you'd swear he was in a coma. So one day out of four or five peace would reign, and then the whole thing would start over again. His new day/night clock was about a hundred hours long. All this I learned from Junior and then Ellen and very little from direct observation. I was never one of the caregivers. That takes a form of heroism that's out of my realm. You couldn't spend any time around the place at that time without knowing what was going on and getting involved on some level.

I wasn't around much. Within a year, Catocho and I were so busy I had had to slack off my work around the cottages, offering to pay the old lady instead. No, she said. I could make up the time. Knew how to calculate interest, did the old girl. I think I'm still catching up. The cottage business took quite a hit, and there were astronomical new expenses since they now needed around the clock caregivers in addition to Junior and the old lady, who, bless their hearts, just weren't up to it. Now the two scorpions had a cobra in the jar with them.

I have to give them credit, though, especially in retrospect. The old man wanted to stay home, and they wanted him to be able to stay at home. They weren't being cheap. It's hard to imagine how the situation could have cost them any more had it been handled any other way. I think they went through about a dozen caregivers before the situation settled down, which only happened after Ellen came on the scene. I saw one of the would-be caregivers fly out of the driveway so fast you'd swear she'd been shot out of a cannon. I heard the old man tell another one, "Don't blame me if I bite you." Junior always looked like he'd just gone a few rounds of some particularly dirty brand of boxing through that whole year. The only one who stuck with them start to finish and stayed on in a much more low-key role with the old lady is a Mexican woman named Elbia who'd been their one-day-a-week cleaning gal and who was just very devoted to the old couple, allowing this new role to evolve. I think all three of them would have keeled over long before Ellen arrived if it hadn't been for Elbia. I wish I could spend a chapter or two singing her praises; what a wonderful human being. Somehow she hung in there through those first few months when the old boy was refusing to take any medication.

I'm no advocate of over-medication; no advocate of medication at all if it can be avoided, but if anybody was a candidate for the happy juice, it was old Harold. Initially he took nothing for pain, of which he had plenty. Nothing to help him sleep; nothing to cool down the hallucinations that were cropping up, at least in part, thanks to all that insomnia. Wouldn't even take aspirin. They were all just trying to kill him. He'd bite. He'd throw things. He'd howl through the night. Even though he was rapidly losing the ability to walk, he otherwise remained amazingly strong. I tried to keep my distance, but there was just no getting away from it. I even started feeling sorry for Junior who tried to be there for him and who caught the full force of his fury, lightning rod that he was.

And then Ellen came on the scene, and it was as though the cavalry had arrived, the storm passed, the seas calmed—rode up on her white charger and everything changed, as though everyone knew things were going to be all right. I was only able to see all this in retrospect. I hardly saw her the first few months she was here; just a glimpse now and then going in and out. As Groucho might say, I still—but never mind that. No one even knew that she'd come to stay. I remember Junior saying he thought she'd be here a week or two, thinking the old man was dying; here to say her goodbyes and then back to the mainland. Instead she was here to take charge and to stay. She arrived and everything changed; that's how it looks from a distance. That's how it looks if you don't know better: presto chango. Magic. Junior's reaction was typical: They always did like Ellen better. Ellen always was their favorite. I was insufficiently sympathetic. Can you blame them, Junior? It was true, you couldn't blame them. It was impressive not because it was magic. It was impressive because magic had nothing to do with it. She came in and made things happen. Made changes. The old man did respond differently to her. He still recognized people. He knew who she was. Sometimes he was clear-headed enough to be concerned about how she could manage it; about what she was leaving behind.

I understood about that. "It was time," was about all she'd say back then. This situation was what had brought her back, but it was time. *It was time. I was done there.* How many volumes are contained in those few words and what life doesn't have both the volumes and the few words to describe it, and the desire, the fervent wish to leave it at the few words? She clues me in to the particulars in her own way and in her own time as she sees fit. Lord knows I reproach her often enough for having lived this high-powered career on the mainland for fifteen years and not even having become a billionaire. The nerve. As to the other obvious question, I myself can't imagine why she became interested in me. On that score I'm no help. She arrived in the fall, about a year after I did, and we barely saw each other for the first six months, only crossing paths with a wave and a few words now and then. She kept her things in Number 11, at the other end of this row, and she went there to nap and catch her breath once in a while, but she was spending all her time in the big house.

Getting old Harold to accept the fact that he was going to have to take medication was the first big hurdle. They were all in agreement that he wasn't to be tricked or deceived about medication. You have to applaud them. I can only imagine the temptation. After all it was for the man's own good. It was only through Ellen's persistence that he came around, and even with that, it took a long time. At first she was just the latest one trying to poison him. She had to take the stuff herself once or twice in his presence to convince him otherwise, which I'm not advocating, by the way, and neither would she. In fact, I suspect she'd be pretty annoyed that I'm even mentioning it here. Even when old Harold was convinced, or at least satisfied that he wasn't being poisoned, he wasn't convinced for long. Then she had the endless and excruciating process of figuring out which medication to use and at what dosage and in combination with which other and what dosage for that. The doctors weren't in agreement, to say the least. Someone very observant had to be monitoring how things were working day by day. It's a tricky business. A medication will work for a while and then not; maybe the dosage has to be changed; maybe side effects start to kick in; maybe the side effects only kick in with the interaction of medications over long periods. I tell her she missed her calling; she could give a course to med students, if not doctors, at this point. She takes a humbler position; says her experience is based on one patient. You can't generalize. Whether she'd make it a second career or would even go through it again only she knows. Splendid but overwhelmingly unknown territory is the human mind, that's all I know. To trot out the old cliché: the most extraordinary unexplored territory in the universe is the terrain between two ears. It also happens to be where all the silver in the mine is buried; where all the Golden Geese are hatched.

The situation took its toll on all of them, as I've said. Even from my perch in Number 14 I could tell. I look at the result—again I have to tip my hat. Within six months after Ellen's arrival, old Harold was comfortable and calm the vast majority of the time. His caregivers were on a regular schedule. Even the family members took shifts. They were able to get some rest. He got outside a lot where he did best and stayed at home, the home and grounds he'd built. He stayed home until he died a couple of years later. It's about the best we can hope for.

By the way, if I left the impression that Junior had dropped his lawsuit because of all of this or at least with all of this going on, let me correct the impression. His version of this part of the narrative went something like this: of course, he was happy to have his kid sister around again, but he had gotten the situation under control long before she'd arrived. It was fine that she was getting all the credit—very magnanimous that Junior—but it was just more evidence of what he'd always said: his folks had always shown a marked contrapatrilineal favoritism when it came to the two of them. That was his lingo, his creativity at work: contrapatrilineal favoritism. Think I could make that up? The alliance that developed between Ellen and me had the clear earmarks of a coalition to thwart his ends. That's jumping ahead a bit. That's clearly how he came to view things.

For once in this dreary narrative I can focus on something positive, and I can't let Junior's warped perspective spoil it. First of all, if I haven't yet mentioned what I did after work, it's because what I mostly did after work was stare at the back of my eyelids until the next morning. By the time I moved out here, I was in my late thirties. Okay, my extremely late thirties. Until we started working for St. Pete, it was unusual to get back to the cottages before six or seven at night, particularly during the long daylight hours. A big night out was going over to Puppy Palace for Chinese takeout. That's where the chapter titles come from, as I think I've mentioned. They have some excellent fortunes in their cookies. Just recently I opened a couple of others I might have liked to include. Runners-up. One went, "A clear conscience is usually the sign of a faulty memory." Pretty good. Wish I had a spot for it. Another went, "We are taught by every person we meet." You see, they have a knack for sayings that seem utterly innocuous and even insipid, but on closer inspection are anything but. Another goes, "Over every mountain there is a path, although it may not be seen from the valley." I decided that one sounds like a cliché without actually being a cliché, which makes it even better.

Puppy Palace is on the main road between here and Sterling, about eight miles away. It has another name; that's just what I call it. Early on in our friendship, Ellen asked me where the name came from. It's sad when you go there, I told her. You can see right into the kitchen, see all the cages there off to one side, hear all the yapping puppies. You order 'chicken,' the cook comes out holding a cute little white puppy. He holds the puppy up to you and smiles his big smile, looking for your approval. Sometimes he even scratches the little thing under the chin a couple of times and rocks it in his arms as he walks back into the kitchen, still looking back at you once or twice, still smiling, that big cleaver hanging from his belt. You order 'pork', same thing happens, although the puppy might have darker fur. For some reason the cook doesn't do any of that when Ellen goes there. I think she gave me *that* look, or tried to, for the first time, after I told her all this. I say: Asians stop eating dogs; I stop calling it Puppy Palace.

Joseph M. Mascia

This all points out what's sure to be the second big disappointment concerning this narrative. The first, in case you didn't notice, is that, despite the setting on an island with a celebrated history of whaling and commercial fishing and rum-running and sea exploits of all kinds, boats and fish and whales and rum don't figure in the story in the least. Barely a glancing mention here and there. The second concerns parties and riotous living in general. This is, after all, one of the places where big shots have been coming to get loaded and act stupid for decades. Not right here, but on the island. But it's as though the characters on these pages inhabit a different planet. Well, there it is. No wild parties here start to finish. There was the ending of that dream, I suppose, if you want to count that. Fancy cooking to me meant opening up two different kinds of canned soup, combining the contents, and actually heating it up before eating. Not that I don't like a good meal or can't cook—just too tired, usually. Evenings involved a few minutes looking over some plans, a few phone calls, a few pages of a good book, then out cold. Had I been in on everything going on in the big house, I could never have done my work during the day. The days I kept free for odd jobs around the cottages were like days off in comparison with most days, which combined hectic and somewhat hazardous with physically exhausting.

It sometimes happened that I would find some daylight left after a supper of leftover puppy, and I'd stroll down to the dock to watch evening settle in. The dock was rarely used even when families were renting in the summer. It had, then as now, about twenty feet of walkway and then one larger float, which is about ten feet square. Not ten square feet. Ten feet on a side. The float stays out year round—waves are largely absent here in the harbor pond. Even when it freezes over, it rarely breaks up with the ferocity you'll see along the open shoreline. So the dock, so far, prevails, preserving in its construction and repairs its share of the intramural skirmishes between father and son.

2.

It was on the dock that Ellen and I first became acquainted, beyond the passing greetings we'd shared to that point. I would be done for the day, but she, more often than not, would be gearing up for what was sure to be a sleepless night. Her beverage then would be black coffee. Mine would be anything cold she wanted to offer me: water or ginger ale or sometimes something wild like a beer or white wine on ice. It turns out that we both had at these times the overwhelming desire that time simply move more slowly. It's the sensation that still characterizes our time together: we just want more of it. As low key as possible.

Sometimes we'd talk about music. Then we started listening to music. She had a tiny CD player that ran on batteries that we toted down to the dock. We were like kids at the beach back in the old days, back in olden times, sitting around a transistor radio. I admit I hadn't thought much about the woodwind instruments before I met her. More accurate to say I hadn't thought much of them. Obviously, I'm talking about my preconceptions, my misconceptions at the time. It's been an education, to say the least, being around that kid. I had listened to plenty of classical music by then. What can I say? Get bombarded by enough of what passes for music at construction sites, you run for the alternative. I loved the music of Dvorac, for example, almost all of it, except for an orchestral piece he wrote for wind instruments. Don't ask me why. I just didn't like it; still don't. Maybe I had indigestion the first time I listened to it. Who knows? So she brought out a CD of his serenade for strings, arranged for and played by wind instruments. That I liked. I mentioned to her once that I found the lead wind part, I can't remember at the moment whether it's oboe or clarinet, in a piece by Strauss to be kind of goofy. It's one of his tone poems, about a trickster type character from European folk tradition. Poor guy gets it in the neck. The whole piece has a sort of darkly humorous feel to it. Anyway, there's a prominent part for one of the wind instruments—probably the oboe, now that I think of it—and the part just strikes me as goofy. I like the music well enough. That's just the association that grew in my mind: when a composer wants goofy or whimsical, he trots out the oboe. So she brought out a CD of a late work by Strauss for oboe and orchestra. "See what you think of this," she said. Lots, it turned out. There was a wind quintet by Barber that doesn't seem to be played much on classical radio, at least in comparison with some of his other pieces, but like some of his other works, every time you hear it you want to focus in; you hear more. Then there was Brahms. I'd heard plenty of Brahms. She introduced me to his late works for winds. Suffice to say that 'goofy' is no longer the first word that comes to mind when I think of the oboe or clarinet.

Now Ellen, on the other hand—but this calls to mind another aspect of our informal, hopefully endless music seminars: she takes her playing very seriously. She was good when she got out here. She's very good now. She quips that it would be more remarkable for someone who practices three hours a day *not* to improve, but that false modesty thing cuts no ice with me. Listening to music on the radio or on a little CD player is one thing. Listening to it as it was meant to be heard, and in my case, sitting right next to the person playing it, or at least working on it—something else altogether. She started inviting me to Ponnack Harbor to the old opera house where the orchestra gives most of its performances. In the summer they give a few outdoor concerts. They've been invited to perform further afield. They've managed it a few times. They're not professionals, though they pick up some paying gigs, and I think lots of the individuals in the orchestra could be pros. Words can't possibly capture it—listening to some of the best music ever written, well played, in a venue with good acoustics—at least I can't possibly find the words to capture it. Why try to write about music, anyway? When there's music. Any description in words of a piece of music I've ever come across seemed at best about as close to the mark as, say, a mathematical formula approximating a waterfall. When you're at the concert, you're riding the waterfall. Without a barrel. And you live to tell the tale. And the tale you tell is sure to be banal and insipid, at least in comparison to the actual experience. You see? Descriptions fail and analogies fail. Life was taking a dramatic turn for the better; I'll leave it at that.

There's a trail that more or less follows the shore all the way from this property around the neck of the harbor and out to the open beach on the bayside. It's a trail that predates almost all the other houses on this side. Somehow it's remained. It's not a long walk—maybe a mile and a half to the harbor inlet, the jetty and the beach. When she didn't have to get back in a hurry, when the days were longest, we'd sometimes make the trek. When it's clear weather, you can see over to the mainland very low on the horizon from the jetty or the beach. On Friday nights in the summer, at least half a dozen locations on the far shore have fireworks displays. Our daughter loves to watch the brilliant bursting lollipops of color far away across the water where all the tiny people live. It was one of the things that we got into the habit of doing early on; takes our minds off all the tiny people on this side, I guess.

One night that first summer, our first summer, we sat watching as one by one the Lilliputians over there shot off their grand finales. As we got up and helped each other slap the sand off our pants, I guess I just had to say something stupid. I said, with things all stabilized with the old man she'd soon be able to go back to her exciting life on the mainland, the land of fireworks, and that would be it for me, the old mudslinger. Woe is me, kind of thing. She started to scoff at the notion that Junior and her mom could handle old Harold without her, then stopped herself mid-thought and just stared at me. Just kept staring at me from real close. Then she turned and looked across the water for not nearly as long, then turned back to me. "There's nothing over there for me," she said. Then she came very close.

That night pretty much settled things between us. That's also about as wild as this narrative gets, by the way. I remember that another thought crossed my mind as we stood there together, or shortly thereafter: this will cost you, I thought, the thought aimed at myself, not her. And I wasn't thinking of money. I didn't know myself what I meant by it. I remember thinking, too, that it was a peculiar thought to have at such a moment. It's come back to me more than once recently, in an entirely different context. Heavy costs all around.

I wouldn't have stayed, I'm sure of that; I wouldn't have stayed much beyond that first year. Why would I have stayed there among those vipers? Ellen was as unlike her brother as it's possible for two people to be, in any way you choose to compare. Doesn't really resemble any of them. Who was delivering the milk back then? Of course, I see the family resemblance to both her folks. No, she doesn't have her dad's little moustache. She's not hard to look at; I'll leave it at that. She's got the long, lean athletic part, too. Her mom was athletic, too, as I understand it, in her own way. A trained ballerina and gymnast in her youth. An effortless, beautiful swimmer is Ellen. It's something else we have in common: she loves to swim; I love to watch her swim. I think I've mentioned, I can't remember where, that crossing the harbor pond and back is a good healthy swim. Or, as Groucho might say, a good unhealthy swim if the bilge is flowing this way. Anyway, it's over a mile round trip, and I've seen her do it twice and then go on with her day as though it had been nothing more strenuous than a stroll. She doesn't do any competitive sports, but she could win those kinds of contests where they swim long distances across stretches of open water.

They don't do those out here because, between the chop and the currents, they'd lose about half the contestants. I've been caught in the cross-shore currents while skin diving—an extraordinary feeling, like a conveyor belt and no getting off. An old fish-head told me that if you get caught in a certain current, you might finally pull out of it about six hundred yards off shore. Ah, well then.

When she swims, she thinks of music, she says, thinks of Brahms, thinks of Elgar. Thinks of pieces she's working on, goes over the passages, over and over in her mind, working them out. Doesn't make them any easier to play, necessarily, she says, just a wonderful experience.

I hate to bring Junior back into it when things were finally looking up, but this incident occurred a little later the same summer that Ellen and I started our coalition, our sinister alliance, and there's no getting around it. As I've mentioned, given the work I was doing, getting to sleep at night wasn't exactly a problem. If I needed or wanted to stay awake in the evening, that could be a problem. On occasion it did happen that I'd be preoccupied and a little restless, and so, often as not on those occasions, I'd walk down and sit on the dock, looking west towards the harbor and the marinas. All the water nearby is salt or brackish, so there aren't many mosquitoes.

On this particular night, the breeze off the ocean hadn't died down. It was warm, almost hot. Ellen was in the big house. I sat there utterly quiet, content to be awake, then lay down, arms under my head. Things around had grown quiet. The whole town is that way, other than summer weekends along the hotel row. That can get pretty lively, I'm told. In general, it's a family town. It goes to bed early. Just that day a new family had moved into Number 2 for the week. It's the closest cottage to the dock—a good stone's throw away up a gentle rise. They'd long since gone to bed. All their lights were off. There was no moon. There were high clouds, no fog, but very dark. I was getting ready to pack it in before I fell asleep and woke up sore all over when all at once it sounded as though some large animal was crawling out from underneath Number 2, trudging across the lawn in my direction. My heart gave a leap. I couldn't imagine what it was. There are plenty of stray cats around, but this was far larger than a stray cat. We have lots of deer. They'll come out of the woods towards evening to work the lawns and the more succulent shrubs, particularly those on which homeowners have spent a fortune. I know what they sound like when they come around, and to my knowledge they don't crawl around under the cottages. There are no bears on the island other than the stock market variety. Then I saw that all too familiar form in dim silhouette, that stooped, lumbering gait as he trudged back to the big house and disappeared from view. Then, once again, complete silence.

Back in my own familiar Number 14, where I sit at the moment before the hearth, I was awake quite a while longer as I thought about it. I was distracted and preoccupied by it the whole next day. I didn't say anything to Catocho, who was about the only person I said anything to that day, though it called to mind his snap judgment of Junior, a judgment he'd made almost before they'd said a word to each other. "He strange," he'd said in his distinctive English way back then, elaborating a little in his Spanish, which was equally distinctive and idiosyncratic. No college degrees, no titles or letters after his name, but no fool.

Now I had a dilemma on my hands. Strange is one thing. Criminally sick is another. Loser is one thing. Candidate for prison time is another. Any contractor can amuse you with stories of conversations innocently overheard or scenes inadvertently witnessed while working in or under a house, some of which have at least a grain of truth to them. Whatever Junior was up to didn't fall into that category. Nothing inadvertent or innocent about it. Nor was this just a stupid juvenile indiscretion. As it was the first I'd witnessed and I wasn't even sure what I'd witnessed, I decided on direct person-to-person confrontation. Humiliation, really, in plain English. Whatever my strikes before this, this was clearly my third. It was all up with me after that. I have to admit that the way I spoke to Junior after this incident, the way I treated him, differed only in degree with the way I'd treated him previously. Once I hold someone in contempt, I treat him with contempt. I can't help it. There is only one type of authority: moral authority, of which he had none. He was nothing; a creature with no spine, a worm, an insect. True I'd have to continue to deal with him in any number of ways, but I could only pity him for the degenerate malformed creep that he was, as if he were some helpless, hopeless creature.

The next day I went over to the panel of skirting that accessed the crawl space under Number 2 and screwed it shut with a great excess of deck screws. I ran a string with tin cans attached around my cottage, only mine. When he came near enough with inquiring, suspicious looks, I shouted to him that I suspected that a rat or a weasel was crawling around under the cottages, but not to worry, if I caught it—I drew one finger across my throat. He marched off without saying a word or looking at me directly, though his face turned that rare shade of purple I'd seen it take on before. His expression was sour but determined as I'd seen in those with no capacity for self-doubt or reproach, those for whom blame is always and forever elsewhere.

As I say, I was done for and should have known it then and there. I left the matter there; didn't tell anyone else, removed my strings and cans a few days later though I left it for him to remove the deck screws from the panel of skirting. Until these lines are found, I still haven't told anyone else.

3.

Harold Senior's condition stabilized, but he continued on a slow downward slide. Ellen's plans for our wedding went ahead; it was to be held on the grounds the next spring. They were her plans, mostly, and I hoped it went well for her sake. Keep it small, was my contribution, which I repeated as often as I thought I could get away with. I needn't have worried; her plan was elegant as I would have anticipated. She did keep it small, for which I was grateful. May. She was taking a chance holding it outdoors in May. May can feel like March with an unlucky roll of the dice, but she wanted old Harold to be there and as lucid as possible, and she felt his condition was deteriorating month by month. Monitoring his condition month by month and day by day was her department. I could never have made that call. Plan B was to all squeeze into the living room of the big house with its wall of picture windows overlooking the harbor and the fireplace with all the smoldering tires.

We caught a break with the weather: sunny and breezy. Windbreaker weather, nothing more. It couldn't have worked out better and who wasn't happy for Ellen that beautiful day? I don't think there was anyone who saw Ellen with her old man that day who wasn't moved. She had hired the principal violinist, violist, and cellist from her orchestra, and as she came in with old Harold, leading him in with the wheelchair, they played their own arrangement of a few movements from the Enigma Variations. I swear it left everyone, including me, melted into a little puddle on the lawn. He wore that big grin the whole time, not even on the happy juice, just smiling for his girl. No outbursts. You could see that he got it. He didn't say a word, but his silence couldn't have been more eloquent. Father Pat said a few good words to the effect that he had his doubts about me, but he knew good men were scarce, so we all had to trust Ellen's judgment and hope for the best. I couldn't have agreed more. There was Junior in his ill-fitting suit, trying his best not to scowl, though I think by this time he'd forgotten how to smile. Biding his time. There was the old lady with her amazingly blond hair and her skin two notches too tight. I know for a fact she could no longer smile. There was Catocho and his wife and her sister and her husband and their kids. Catocho hadn't even tried to get into a suit jacket—there isn't a tailor alive who could modify a coat off the rack to fit him properly—but he was all slicked up. Had on his dazzling, pointy boots in case anyone needed to be flogged and evicted. There was the Baass who'd flown in to be best man, as I've already mentioned. He'd lost the little ponytail since I'd seen him last. Not much between him and heaven now, as they say. He always was ahead of me in everything.

Then there's Ellen, of course, and how she looked. Not difficult to look upon is my *corazon*; nor even to listen to. I'll have to leave it at that because if I start rhapsodizing I may never be able to force myself to get back to the business at hand. We moved into Number 2 where we still live and held onto Number 14 where we store things and I have an office and she practices the oboe and clarinet and even then I would often sit here scribbling at night so that she'd accuse me of visiting old Mrs. Matalonis in Number 9 and I'd say, how else can I get even for all those Coast Guard boys she entertains over in Ponnack Harbor when she claims to be practicing with the orchestra? No more eating out of cans for me. Nor Puppy Palace, unless we're feeling nostalgic and hankering for a stomachache. We've kept my little place up in the White Mountains where we spent part of the honeymoon week and where we get away now and then. It's a good antidote to the island. Thoroughly rustic. Okay, a hovel, if you have to have it straight. That's its nickname. A cabin that was on the property when I bought the land over a decade ago. Everyone should have a hovel.

A little scary the way things seemed to be working out. I've always been a little suspicious of success. People start smiling too much when you're doing well. When you're struggling, they tell you what they really think. It's as though your own difficulties serve to unshackle their words and actions; allow them to unsheathe their claws. Kind of like old Harold. When you're down, people feel free to let 'er rip.

By the spring of the wedding, we'd already done a few jobs for St. Pete, and he was talking about taking us on full time, while still leaving us time around the margins for side jobs. This was, as construction jobs go, a dream possibility and not even to be thought about, since thinking about it would feel like torture. Yet there it was. The year after the wedding it came to pass. Good pay; good jobs; time off. No more scrambling to get enough work; to get paid; to keep Catocho busy. I had to pinch myself. Scary how it brought me back. I looked forward to getting up in the morning again—almost. By then, by the year of the wedding, no longer even close to being in my extremely late thirties, I was feeling it. Here was a man who actually wanted you to knock off at a reasonable time. We put more pressure on ourselves than he put on us. Given the work, he made sure the working conditions were as humane as possible.

Time off—what a concept. I could farm out Catocho, my little red bull. Who didn't appreciate his help? I could still fit in work at the cottages; start to ease up. There would be no end to it. St. Pete's business was booming, and he loved construction projects. He was taking his business public. It would be earning him many multiples of what he now brought in. He would be taking us with him. We'd all have as much work as we could handle for the rest of our working lives. Once he was done with the—dozens and dozens—of houses he needed for family, extended family, help, visiting clients; or concurrently—concurrently, of course— there would be investment properties that we, the nail-bangers and mudslingers could buy into if we were able and inclined.

Junior with his painting company was one of the contractors St. Pete fit in around the margins but, as often as not, his role fell into the category of comic relief. His roles had always been modest: deck refinishing, staining, trim painting. Often he was the one to limit his crew's involvement. St. Pete wasn't, after all, a Golden Goose. Merely a second stringer. Junior would keep some time available, he said. You have to wonder why he added the part about painting emergencies. Always just asking for it. In the event of a true 'painting emergency' he could be counted on. Sounded okay until you thought about it for a while. *Painting emergency?* When in the history of civilization, in the history of the human race, had there been a painting emergency? After that, painting emergencies cropped up everywhere on the St. Pete job sites and for a long time, and when things got tense or ugly, all anyone had to do was call out a painting emergency requiring Junior's immediate presence and everyone's mood improved. Even when he had no work on the house, he was a frequent visitor. He was checking on me, of course, his traitor, his betrayer, the one who owed it all to him; ostensibly there to inquire about when I'd get to this or that job at the cottages or some project for him, but his visits increasingly took on a more sinister quality. The others would come to me and say things like, "He says you're spreading lies about him. He says you can't be believed or trusted." Paranoid, of course. I never told any of those guys about—his strangeness. His possibly criminal strangeness. I never even told Ellen. That's my fault, of course, and soon this gets buried. I've always thought there was one surefire way to avoid mental anguish and that's to—not—do things you're ashamed of. That doesn't work for psychopaths, of course, who aren't ashamed of anything, and I know it's too simplistic. Just a good rule of thumb for good people. Should be on another fortune cookie.

Junior wasn't a psychopath. He was, increasingly, a sick man. In retrospect, his health problems seem a particularly cruel business, coming right on the heels of the old man's illness, and I sometimes wonder now how many of the foolish things he said and did in his last few years were just his illnesses talking; you know, to trot out the old cliché, the encephalopathy kicking in. I'm not making excuses for him, particularly given that I was the one he was trying to do in. It just comes to mind now that the smoke's cleared and some time has passed.

I think that boil on his butt was the first thing that landed him in the hospital. After that it was like a cascade, like the floodgates had been opened. I remember visiting him on one of his job sites where he had a couple of his guys doing yard work. They'd trudge back and forth from the lawn to the nearby oak woods dragging tarps full of leaves deep into the woods. I told him to be sure to tell his guys that Lyme disease was no joke; that they should check themselves for ticks later. Words to that effect. His response, in essence was, good, I hope they get it. Not, "Good, ha-ha, hope they get it, ha-ha." Just, "Good, hope they get it." Serious. Insufficiently awestruck in his presence were the Josés, no doubt. Insufficiently under thumb. Not long after that Junior isn't feeling well himself and goes in for some blood work. It turns out that he has Lyme and that he's had it for some time—years probably. It's so deep seated they don't think they can root it out. They try. Put him on massive doses of antibiotics for months. It wasn't long after this that he started talking about his spastic colon. Now don't imagine that I don't understand the seriousness of all the maladies that can afflict every square inch of our poor organisms or that I'd take pleasure in ridiculing someone for afflictions they suffer. Why, though? Why did he have to come onto St. Pete's job site and talk about his spastic colon as though there was nothing else in the world you wanted to hear about and in excruciating detail? So that you couldn't help but speculate afterwards that perhaps some mischievous cabal, some devious coalition of MDs, in prescribing all those antibiotics, just happened to neglect to tell him, perhaps under the assumption that since he knew all things, he'd be sure to know this, that all those antibiotics would wipe out every living thing in his gut, without which we can't digest much, and so he'd be virtually turning himself inside out every time he sat on the toilet, until he complains to this mischievous bunch who scratch their heads and their chins and shake their heads, seemingly mystified as they walk away until they round a corner and then fall to pieces, rolling on the floor, slapping each other on the back, drooling and choking with laughter. Pure, idle speculation, and entirely unlikely, but you just couldn't help yourself after a while, the way he kept bringing this stuff up.

His afflictions kept piling up, and he kept right on assuming that everyone wanted nothing more than to hear all about it. There was no use trying to get a word in edgewise. Whatever your problem or your wife's or your child's or your uncle's, he had you beat. He could top it. It was true, too. After a while, you had to step back and acknowledge the obvious. The man was the master of misery. It turned out, for example, that his was no garden variety, Lyme-induced arthritis, but had progressed to bone-on-bone hip pain, for which he was prescribed heavy-duty pain killers, which made him even loopier and, if possible, more self-absorbed. It further turned out that his hips were inoperable, were un-replaceable, since with his Hep C, it was feared he wouldn't be able to fight off the infections that might follow the operations. About the time he started bringing up his Hep C, which chronologically was pretty late in the game, speculation ran to whether it wouldn't be more humane to take the poor slob out back and shoot him. Undoubtedly, there's altogether too much time for idle speculation on a job site, particularly late in the afternoon with no power tools running.

By the late stages, St. Pete no longer wanted Junior on his job sites or even to come by for his formerly welcomed visits. It had nothing to do with the work his men did or sympathy or lack thereof for his multitude of health woes. It's as though St. Pete read the man, his toxicity. The medicated one, he called him. He never ridiculed or belittled anyone. He just didn't want Junior around anymore. This judgment reminds me of Catocho's and had, I think, much the same basis. Catocho made no bones about the causes of Junior's health woes. "Bad spirit. Bad spirits," he'd say. I don't go there. Once you take that route it's far too easy to find outcomes to match your preconceptions. As I say, such accounts never tally. Virtue is a poor predictor of comfort and wellbeing.

Then there was Junior's coalition, also pretty late in the game. To drive me off the island, apparently. Who the hell knows? They'd call me up and tell me about it almost as soon as he said it to them; his coalition. Like OPEC. They couldn't contain themselves. The man was too much.

I still felt sorry for him. Now I was really stuck with him and vice versa. I had to deal with him at the cottages. On occasion I continued to fit his jobs in, believe it or not. Don't ask me why. In retrospect—what good is retrospect now? How far back should I go? What should I undo? I pitied him, so I didn't rat on him. I pitied him, so I tried to help him—in my own way. It all rings so hollow. I know I have to keep putting one foot in front of the other. There's so little time left.

There was another incident that occurred during the same year as the wedding, that same spring in fact, about a month later. I was on a small job, one of Junior's, one of his Wannabees. Out in the woods between Sterling and Ponnack. I had set Catocho up somewhere else. I don't remember now just where. I could figure it out if I dug up my old calendar. I save that old crap for some reason. Here's a reason. And I don't even bother. Where was Catocho? Doesn't matter. Not with me. I was working alone. I drove to a deli for lunch. I was driving back to the site. In front of me was some kind of light-colored compact car—white or off white. The road is windy out there; that's windy as in up and down and left and right. Dense woods. Lots of houses. People drive way too fast out here, out there, everywhere on the island, but we weren't. Neither he nor I. He was just toodling along. I was a safe distance behind him. There was a girl up ahead standing by the side of the road, off to the side, but in the lane of travel. Not a young girl; late teens. Dressed for the warm day: shorts and a tee shirt. She crouched to pick something out of the road as the car ahead of me approached. Unbelievably, she made no move to lunge away. Unbelievably, the car neither slowed nor swerved. It was as though she didn't exist. I distinctly remember that she turned her head to face the car as it reached her, still down in a crouch, then she seemed to explode out of that crouch, to fly, to be thrown, as if you took a rag doll by one leg and tossed it across a room. She landed facedown in the ditch beside the road. The car that hit her rolled to a stop. I pulled my truck off the road and knelt by her side, looking for a pulse. An off-duty cop pulled up soon. He was in the neighborhood and responded first to the call. We turned her over. She was still breathing, but there was nothing to be done. I supported her head so that her breaths could come more easily. They were whispered sighs with a note in each breath. She was breathing her last as the ambulance arrived.

There wasn't a peep in the island's newspaper, though a brief report with a picture was in one of the mainland papers. The journalist seemed to make up a lot of the details. They had little to do with the scene I'd witnessed and I was the only eye witness. The driver, it turns out, was ill, on oxygen, medicated. He hadn't even seen the girl, as I had guessed. He had to be taken to the hospital himself from the sheer shock and stress of it. Never saw her. They had a picture of the girl, some girl there in the paper. She had a pale, northern complexion, like an Irish girl, though with dark hair and eyes, a rather long pretty face. The girl who died in my arms was darker, like Catocho, with classic Mayan features. She'd been struck directly in the forehead but her face was still there and her lovely facial structure. She was as pretty as the girl in the picture, only different.

Someone puts a wreath on a nearby telephone pole; new ones every so often. It's unlikely that I would happen to cross paths with the person who does it, and why should I intrude upon a mother's grief? Let it go. I still have no answers to the questions that arose from that day. Even assuming the girl in the picture and the girl there in my arms were one and the same, I still have so many questions. For her especially.

Old Harold lived another full year after the wedding; long enough to be introduced to his granddaughter. How he smiled. He had stopped talking months before. Rarely any outbursts that whole last year. No more medication issues. He died at home, in bed. I built a memorial here in a quiet corner of the property: a handful of boulders arranged informally—a little abstract. I thought of tinkering with it from time to time; then decided to let it stand. Sometimes the rough first thought is fine without endless tinkering.

Junior finally shut up about his lawsuit, though he never officially dropped it as far as I know. I was the new enemy after all. I was the new thwarter of all his schemes and ambitions, his nocturnal missions. A rhyming couplet. There'll be sonnets! There'll be sonnets after all. In case it might be imagined that I had or have any ambitions of my own regarding this place, I should point out that my name is on nothing here except the marriage license. If I were to go, I'd go with my tools and my truck and enough cash for the boat ride. That, as the saying goes, was how things stood while things were still standing. Now I know exactly how, in what manner I would go, or rather, be led away. Until Ellen came on the scene, my ambition regarding this place was to leave it. Junior had nothing to fear from me; that was just the direction his thoughts took. Of course, I kept tabs on him; monitored him somewhat. What else could I do under the circumstances? All he needed to do was grow up. Seems he couldn't quite manage it. You know, you look back and think, what was the big deal? Why such a tempest in a teapot? Why did it all happen? The world shrugs and moves on.

It was Ellen who kept me here, just as the thought of her and our daughter now keeps me putting one foot in front of the other. Towards the end, with Harold Senior, I'd be with her more often in the big house; with them. I'd see him go from barely alive to alert and beaming, sitting up. Alive and interested. She had entered the room. He had heard her voice. I watched as, in his last month, unconscious in any usual sense of the term, with one of the caregivers, he'd pick at his clothing; no longer able to speak coherently, he would mutter his comments on his dream state. His eyes, by then, saw only this parallel world of his mind's own creation. She would enter the room, and he'd come back; become silent; calm; listening intently; to her voice. Eyes closed, he'd reach for her hand, hold and stroke her hand; bring her hand up against his cheek; bring her hand to his lips.

She plays an ethereal piece in the first light of morning. Through the fog it draws me to her, her notes weaving and swirling with the tiny droplets. The girl who danced for joy with her shadow whenever the sun came back after a long absence.

Chapter Seven

"Everything Is Not Yet Lost."

1.

*C*OALITON. *WHAT MADNESS.* To drive me off the island. This after I was married into his family. This after Catocho and I were essentially working full-time with St. Pete's crew and turning down the vast majority of offers that came our way from all sides: homeowners and contractors we'd worked for previously and others who'd heard of and seen our work through all of the above. So they came to me and told me all about it almost immediately: his coalition. Laughing to beat the band. Could you believe this guy? No, you really couldn't. He was too much. Just too good. The gift that kept on giving. The Golden Goose that kept on laying golden eggs; the inventive genius who kept on launching lead balloons. They were a great disappointment to him, his coalition. After all he'd done for them. After all they owed him. To stab him in the back like this. So he'd have to take matters into his own hands. If you want something done right—can't get good help these days. So I imagine.

I'm extrapolating; assuming. Based on the events that followed. Who wants to try to get inside that spider's lair between his ears? I had him trapped in his own lair. Whose fault was that? Had I sought the role? If I kept tabs on him a little, if I monitored him to some extent, what else was I supposed to do under the circumstances? It wasn't even much of a predicament, when you got right down to it. All he had to do was grow up. Instead he acted like a trapped, wounded animal; instead he lashed out.

St. Pete no longer allowed him on his job sites, as though he didn't want his family, his children to have to breathe the same air. As though his presence would leave some stain or stench that would be virtually impossible to remove. The medicated one was to come around no more. Why did I continue to do side jobs for him? Strictly pity? Keeping tabs? I do not know. Lord knows we didn't need his work. Catocho and I still squeezed in a couple of days a month working on the cottages. After the wedding, Ellen and I paid the old gal full freight for Numbers 2 and 14. In addition to caring for our daughter, Ellen more or less took over running the cottage business for her mom.

In fact, when you gave the matter a second's thought, the obvious way, the only way to have driven me off the island was through Ellen; set some female trap for me here at the cottages. There were strangers coming through the place almost on a weekly basis. Perhaps he knew enough not to try; knew it would never work. Perhaps he just wasn't up to that: to overt foul play on that level. His strengths lay elsewhere. He would try to scare me; to show me he was still a force to be reckoned with.

The first incident was seemingly so trivial and innocuous it hardly counts. I never gave it much thought until recently; that it was the first shot. A shot across the bow. I've already described it briefly: the incident with the nail gun. At the time it barely registered. Things happen all the time on construction sites. Things fall. I've had hammers and bricks fall from my scaffolds and come within a few feet of braining someone. You apologize profusely; buy the guy a tool; try to take more precautions. Still things happen. I'm certain he wasn't trying to harm me that day. Junior wasn't one to put a nail or a bullet into somebody. Not even at the end when he was pretty far gone; not even at his most medicated. Most of the time, including the day I'm describing, we got along fine and treated each other civilly. Thinking back on the day—there was no malice in the air. We were just two guys trying to get a little job done. Needless to say, I have no idea what was going on in his head. And I wasn't watching him, obviously. I was looking down, thinking about how we should have been using screws to build those forms. What I imagine went on was that he was in a crouch and started to lose his balance and there was the nail gun in his right hand and there was the back of my head, right handy there to steady himself. That's about the kindest interpretation I can imagine and obviously there's an element of nastiness or threat in the act, even giving it this interpretation. And, as he himself pointed out at the time, luckily his finger wasn't on the trigger. So that was that.

It's analogous in some ways to when two guys are bird hunting side by side and they flush one up to one side and the guy on the wrong side has the better shot, but can't take it. Afterwards he says, could've gotten that one if your damn head wasn't in the way. That happened more than once with me and Baass. Doesn't mean you wanted to shoot your buddy. Sometimes it actually happens. Almost always, it's an accident. I'll admit I gave Junior a little more clearance when he was holding a nail gun after that day, but it was no big deal. I thought about the form boards. I was never one for tossing out perfectly good materials. Contractors mark up the price of materials, so, if they can get away with it, the more they throw out, the more they buy, the more money they make. I never could see it, particularly if it meant tossing perfectly good materials in the dumpster. We saved all kinds of stuff under those decks.

The nail gun incident occurred the year after the wedding, the year Liria was born and Harold Senior died. Junior was very much a sideshow at this point, particularly in the business sense. We hardly did anything for him that year. The forms were for a little patio extension. If the old slab wasn't garbage, we'd pin our new work into it, drilling holes for rebar pins, then, depending on what we were doing, either make a six-inch on center rebar grid or just use screen in the concrete to keep it from cracking. Not screen as in your screen door. They make a heavy wire mesh that comes in rolls, specifically for embedding in concrete. We'd embed the rebar pins as deeply into the old slab as possible, as deeply as we could reasonably drill, anywhere from six inches to as much as a foot. I'd usually do the drilling while Catocho cut the rebar. The cuts didn't have to be too precise so he could handle it. Never got too good with a tape measure, my little red bull. All those tiny lines. For me it meant lots of drilling, lots of horizontal drilling, but the new spline-drive drills made it practical. Made it possible, really. We were always drilling and cutting and otherwise modifying old concrete. At the time I never gave it much thought. We wore gloves and hearing protectors and, whenever we worked in an enclosed space, masks. Colder conditions, heavier gloves. No big deal. It was kind of fun, in fact, if you didn't have to worry about getting paid. No hardship. Just shut your brain off and go. It's just that we did so much of this stuff—drilling and cutting and jackhammering, I started to sense an ominous numbness, not just in my fingers as any carpenter or keyboard operator can tell you about, but throughout my hands and into both forearms. I shrugged it off. Like Junior's nonsense, it was neither here nor there. Maybe a little more rest. Maybe six days a week was pushing it for someone no longer in his extremely late thirties who'd been doing construction for going on twenty-five years. Maybe some of the old contractors were right: I should start to look for someone who could lighten my burden. I already had that. I had good help; as good as it gets, but I could never train him to do what I did. He had his work; I had mine. I could see the way he read my grimaces, the way I shook and shook my hands to try to get some feeling, any feeling back into them. The burning pain was preferable to that eerie numbness. He would lighten my burden in whatever way he could: no longer letting me help him with excavations; no longer letting me move full wheelbarrows; taking over as much of the drilling and cutting and jackhammering as possible. When it came to the more highly skilled aspects of the work, we were stuck. Block work couldn't be avoided, and he couldn't do block work. Don't ask me why. It's not that difficult. We used block backing walls for everything: chimneys and fireplaces and most of our exterior walls other than dry-laid stonework. No avoiding block work for me.

He couldn't do block work without me, but he could do block work with me. He could raise the blocks up into position so that it was only left for me to set them into place, tap them home and clean them up. I knew I was now being carried; needless to say it saddened me. Later just gripping the trowel or a hammer was agony. What could I do then? Watch my tender, my quasi-legal tender, work while I stood around holding a coffee cup? Or listen to the other contractors spin their yarns and air their grievances? Or drive around for materials and to line up jobs and just farm it all out? I suppose that last was the natural progression, the next step. Somehow it didn't appeal. That wasn't where my expertise lay. All this quite late in the day, by the way, starting a couple of years ago. I wasn't used up even then. And until then, what was a little pain and discomfort? Until then I had never set foot in a hospital, other than to visit someone.

Junior's second shot, his second strike, did land me in the hospital, though only for an afternoon, only to get stitched up and test the old coconut a little, to make sure it wasn't cracked, only rattled.

Again the circumstances were ambiguous, and, in retrospect, in hindsight, again I think he wasn't trying to hurt me, just scare me. Another shot across the bow, though this one struck the mast; this one struck the wheelhouse. Or maybe just a plain old accident; we'll never know. I was on hands and knees grouting the stones of a front entry—an open porch—large irregular southwestern sandstone fitted tightly and bordered with cut stone slabs of the same material. Grouting was always about the last thing, other than cleanup. We went back and did all the grouting and jointing once all the stones, or whatever material we were using, had set up, usually at least a day later. It's about the most tedious work imaginable. Once he realized they'd pay us for it, Catocho loved it. On this occasion, I went from lamenting the tedium of the task at hand to experiencing the proverbial blinding white light. Then there was blood dripping down my face and neck, concerned faces and voices around me, 'a short ride in a fast machine,' a brief stay in a top-notch, antiseptic-smelling, remarkably well lighted facility. I had to be told what had happened: I'd been clocked by a two-by-eight that had been left precariously near the edge of the nearly flat roof, left on edge up there for some reason. A windy—that's wind as in gusts and falling objects—day. Nothing to it. Seems someone had seen Junior leave it there about an hour before the incident and shortly before he'd left the site, a fact that for some reason he at first tried to deny. Then he owned up and was even somewhat apologetic. I let it slide. There's plenty of ambiguity there. Things get left on flat roofs, and the winds out here are something to see. Heavier things than two-by-eights get blown off them. Be more careful next time, was all I said. I can ill afford another head injury. As I saw it, there was nothing to forgive him for. These things happen.

Another year passed. A good year all the way around. We were working for St. Pete full time, which as I've pointed out, was about one notch below working directly for the Almighty. At home our little girl had long since taken her first steps and was working on a few words. Then he struck again. His third strike. A little over a year ago now. This time there was no doubting his role or his intention and for one evening I was a lucky man indeed; right up there with Lou Gehrig and the carpenter down in Catocholand. Things had gone from bad to worse health-wise for poor Junior at this point. I think by then the spirochetes had burrowed pretty deeply into his gray matter. He had doctor's appointments for every malady known to mankind and seemed to come up with a new one every time you turned around, his affliction du jour.

It seemed everybody was building. Things had gone from boom to frenzy. I had long since pulled my ad. Now I wanted to unplug the phone. St. Pete was buying more places and drawing up more plans. All his contractors were supposed to gear up and hire additional help. The next spring and thereafter, we'd be booked solid, six days a week, all year, with him alone. Meanwhile we had a little lull with him that winter. One of the jobs was out of state; the permits and other paperwork would take a while.

I had some time to ponder. Gear up. I knew what that meant. I knew how the work was getting done these days, saw the swarms of guys companies were putting on any and every job. Then there was me; there was I, who had routinely done two-man jobs alone and three-man jobs with a little help around the margins and had been going, just out here, six days a week for over five years, finally with good help. I had good help, who spurred me on and bucked me up and went from doing his work to doing his work and half of my work; went from covering for me to carrying me. Now I could no longer touch a trowel or a hammer without searing, stabbing pain that shot up both arms, no longer only at night, so that I finally go to see a specialist who says, in essence, you can have the use of your hands, or you can continue to do this work, but you can't have both. It figured. But Catocho just said, don't worry, *Jefecito*, I continue to do my work and I help you do your work and I get another helper for us so that I can my days beside you spend, to help you place the blocks, and I cut and bring you the stones *como siempre* and, once you choose them, I help you lift them into place, but you have to do that part, *Jefecito*; I will never be able to do that part for you; there is no one who can do that work as you do.

So we'd continue somehow, though I couldn't imagine how. For this man, who had such trust in me and supported his family here and a dozen or more members of his family and extended family back home; and for my own family, obviously, I'd keep going.

Junior, who'd been dubbing along with his painting business for years, was now GCing a house, along with one of his coalition partners—everybody was getting into the act—over in the woods between Sterling and Ponnack Harbor; he'd talked to me about it as far back as the previous fall, practically pleading with me to do the stone-veneer fireplace and two-flue chimney. I didn't know; I'd try, but I couldn't commit. Now even Ellen was bringing it up: how he was saying that I'd agreed to do this thing for him, but was now, as so often before, trying to sabotage all his efforts. Did she really believe that? No, that was just the way he talked, but hadn't I maybe led him on? And hadn't Junior been through an awful lot? And maybe this house would finally get things rolling for him and lead to something— Well, and did she really believe that, either? But I didn't say that part. I explained the situation to St. Pete and his main man, who said, just be ready by the spring, by March, because—yes, I knew—things were gonna fly.

2.

We did Junior's job in the dead of winter, supplying our heat for the inside work and doing our best to close off an area around the scaffolding outside, to cut the wind at least a little. Dear Lord, what a house. Whoever designed it had to be one seriously addled individual. Oh, but to hear Junior describe it, wasn't it just the finest example of this and the latest example of that. I-I Junior. Like the old days again. I was stuck there listening to him for the duration—the longest two months in living memory. Stuck there listening to him, who had gone from fawning and pleading to boasting and browbeating, like the magnificent Mr. Toad, for there we were on his job site, building his fireplace, for his clients, all the time using his driveway and his dumpster and his electricity, until you couldn't help but wonder, what wasn't Junior's? Maybe everything was Junior's? As for his house; the best you could hope for his house was that some future St. Pete—hopefully not too far distant future—would come along and tear the thing down and start over. That's the way it went out here: you were just building sets for their own private movies, their own private stage shows, until the next set of actors showed up and had to have the stage, the set, redone to their own specifications, but amid all the glitz and glitter and froth would be something even the original settlers of any variety would be able to recognize and appreciate and use.

Then he starts in about his schedule and how I'm holding him up, that his framers and his roofers, and his finish carpenters had to be where I was, had to work where I was working, and when would that 'tower of terror' finally be out of his way. Tower of terror. His phrase; he and his framer, for the wood scaffold I've built, tied into the porch roof on which it sits and the house framing on that side; tied in—nailed in to the framing with cleats all around the connection points, and cross-braced, so that it's secure, will never fall, unless the house falls with it, falls first, on which we work securely if not in comfort, without a minute of terror. But let these big shots, these would be big shots, have their joke. He won't rush me. I've been hired to do a job, and I've given a fair price, and it takes as long as it takes. We're working in January and February, and I know that the way to do this job so it's not just a miserable grind is to first study the plans and then say, call me in April, or if you know the circumstances and the people involved, say, call me never. But here we are anyway, in January and February, and it'll get done when winter lets us finish. The roofing that has to be done? That I am standing in the way of? The roof above which we're working; the porch roof that covers an unfinished porch floor and some, for some reason, finished and half-finished porch trim that will all have to be redone anyway since it's gotten soaked repeatedly and all the corners have blown out. So this roof, which protects exactly nothing, is somehow my concern and what's more my problem and my fault, but I won't be rushed anyway. The fireplace and chimney, our project, gets done anyway; despite all the hysteria and histrionics, it gets done.

And then a hard, hard freeze comes in that shuts us down all of one day shy of cleaning things up and tearing down the scaffolding. The weather had been borderline as it was, even using cold weather additives. Now nighttime temperatures dropped to the low teens and below for a few nights in a row. We were holding no one up. When it warmed up for a couple of days in a row, which was looking like next week, we'd finish our capping concrete and pointing and then have the whole scaffold down and out of everyone's way in no time. One more day of a little work on the cap and some acid-washing, and then it's just cleanup and tear down and we can clear out of there and I can sit here staring at the fire and hope and pray that feeling comes back into my hands and arms; sit here and wonder how I'm ever going to get through the coming workload. Anyway, what a relief it would be to be out of there and to be home for a few days; to finally and forever be able to say good-bye to that rancid pile of building materials.

Catocho, who never wants down time, who never kicks back because he has many mouths to feed and, besides, loves his work, is over there still doing cleanup duty inside the house and humping materials for the framers and the trim carpenters, while I catch up on loose ends here at the cottages, which mostly means enjoying some time with my wife and daughter, poking the fire a lot, and reading the paper—two papers—every day. He, Junior, has another job for Catocho to do while I'm home doing nothing. A nothing job for nothing people, says Junior. Not even Wannabees. I'm to tell no one he's even taken on such a job. I-I, Junior. Big shot GC now, is Junior. A good job for Catocho, though. Right up his alley. A foundation to waterproof, along the back wall of a house. Not far from Junior's big project. It'll have to wait, though, until the freeze lets up and the ground fully thaws.

The freeze did ease a little, though not enough to get me back over there, with a light snow that Thursday and temperatures above freezing for a while on Friday. Less than an inch of snow, but it managed to stick around all day Friday. There would be freezing rain that night and then more cold weather that weekend. With any luck we'd finish the job Monday. That Friday afternoon, Junior called from his job site. While I'm home doing nothing, can't I fix the leak around the chimney flashing on Number 5? Can't I come to the site and get my ladder off the porch roof and at least do that? Why did he say that last part, I wonder? About the ladder? It struck me at the time. I recalled it later. It was true: all our ladders—his and mine—were over there. Now why should I drive all the way over there to pick up a ladder to do a twenty-minute caulk job when you're coming back here later? Bring me back a ladder. No, says Junior, he cannot do that. He's going directly to the mainland after work. Won't be back until Sunday. All right, then, it can wait. I'll get the ladder later on and fix the flashing over the weekend. "That's fine," says Junior. That's fine? Junior never says, 'that's fine.' Things for Junior are never fine. Never mind. There's this fire to poke. There's this lovely child whose first steps have evolved into hops and gallops. She is my ambition for the day.

I didn't bother to change before going over there. All I'd be doing was picking up the ladder and then going over to Puppy Palace to pick up dinner. Didn't even change out of my comfy shoes—like slippers, these things. I did my customary deer census on the way: twenty-three living, one dead. Took the roads that would be likely to give me the highest count. No rush. I was losing the light by the time I pulled in the drive, not that it mattered. Friday, late. Late February. Not a soul around. The job site was deserted as well; the framers were getting a good start on getting loaded by now. Junior was off the island already. It suited me fine that nobody was around; I wasn't in the mood to deal with any of them. No ground ladder on our side any more. Someone had borrowed it; now it was locked up with Junior's chain and Junior's padlock in the ladder pile on the far side of the house. Nor had he left a ladder out front for me to pick up. Of course, I had no key to his padlock. There was only one other extension ladder: the one up on the porch roof, tied to our scaffolding. I had to access it through a second-story window, which meant I needed to get into the house. I had brought a screwgun with me to pull the screws from the sheet of plywood that covered the front door opening. Not that there was anything much in there worth stealing. Probably some kind of law by now that a house has to be kept secure, even if there's nothing in it worth securing. The way out to our porch roof from inside the house was through a second-floor back window, then onto the second floor porch around towards our side until the porch ended, then across a short section of first floor porch roof to the corner of the house and, around the corner, six or eight more feet of roof to the point where the ladder leaned against the scaffolding. There was still a layer of snow over there, though it had already melted off the back, south-facing roof. Getting dark already.

Even in the dim light I could see that things weren't the way I'd left them on that roof. As I just mentioned, we usually used a ground ladder to reach the porch roof. From there I'd nailed two-by-four cleats flat to the roof, into the rafters below, nailed parallel to the contour of the roof, just three or four little two-foot long pieces of two-by-four, to use as toe holds until we reached the scaffold ladder. I could see they were gone. I could see the tiny ridges that the new cedar shingles made under the slushy layer of snow. I couldn't see the piece of clear plastic, also under the snow, in my path between the house corner and the ladder. So the shingle boys, the shingleros, had done the porch roof—as much as possible—in our absence. That was brilliant. Water could still get underneath the shingles since they couldn't actually finish the last few courses and the area immediately around the chimney and scaffold. Never mind. Soon enough we'd be out of there. The platform of lumber scraps that leveled up the ladder platform was still there, as was the ladder, as was the scaffold. The ladder was still tied—that's tied as in clothesline, knots— to the scaffolding. I had to cross about eight feet of roof to get to it. No more cleats. The roof wasn't very steep, maybe a four in twelve pitch, but that snow looked awfully slick. Even light frost can make a wood surface slick as sheer ice. Comfy shoes with flat soles: not good. I noticed down near the bottom of the roof the shingleros had left one of their little perches: a two-by-six on edge held in place by pieces of shingle tacked both to it and to the roof using half-embedded roofing nails; flimsy-looking perches. Still they held a surprising cargo. I'd never seen one fail. This one didn't make me feel too secure, twelve feet away down there, the frozen ground about sixteen feet below that. It looked a poor substitute for our sturdy cleats.

Here I have to hand it to Junior. The man had studied his quarry. Any hunter or sniper will tell you: know your quarry. Rule Number One. I had come there to get that ladder. I wanted that ladder. That was my goal for the excursion. I may be wary of success, but I hate failure. Hadn't I expressed the thought in his presence on any number of occasions? Hadn't I amply demonstrated my stubbornness? The man had done his homework. And I had tested the roof; tested my shoes. They held; even on the roof with a little snow on it, they held. Where they didn't hold was on that little piece of plastic lying there minding its own business under the snow. That I hadn't seen. That sent me flying. The other thing about Junior that you have to admire is his patience. This was some sort of subtly diabolical intellect at work. I imagine that if he hadn't gotten me this time, he'd have waited; continued to bide his time; even if it took ten years or the rest of his life; whichever came first. You have to wonder what such a mind might have accomplished, given the right environment, the right conditions. Some new torture, perhaps. They say pathetic, downtrodden, bottom of the pecking order rats made the best Nazis.

It was easy enough for him to justify removing the measures I'd taken to work safely before our job was complete. Situations like that were the norm on jobs where contractors were tripping all over each other. St. Pete's jobs, by contrast, where everybody had the space to work in relative comfort, were the exceptions. Who isn't familiar with accounts of people who imagined they were done for and then somehow escaped their predicament? How long could it have taken between taking that next step and landing on the frozen ground? I could probably figure it out. Assume the roof is a frictionless surface, to simplify things. Roughly twelve feet on the roof; sixteen through the air. Barely a pause while the shingler's perch, which had been cut most of the way through, snaps and comes along for the ride. Add a second for friction. Maybe two or three seconds. I wasn't particularly panicked; didn't see my life pass before my eyes. This is not good. This is surreal. Those might approximate my initial thoughts, plus a few choice expletives that I'll omit, given that this may have to be read aloud in a courtroom. Perhaps I was still thinking of that shingler's perch and how there was a chance it would hold me. Or perhaps I was thinking of that young man, that young Superman who slid down roofs for fun, then grabbed the last rung of the roof ladder, then swung, flopping like a fish on a line, then bounded back onto the roof, shouting, "Never mind. I said, 'Never mind.'" So I would grab that shinglero's perch down there at the edge of the roof, snatch it with one hand, then kick away from the column below, and then I would be back on the roof, standing on that two-by-six perch, shouting "Never mind. Never mind," to the winter night, to the universe, then never give it another thought, not even bother to forgive him, just forget it; forget it like you forget an insect that's stung you. Too bad that hand no longer worked; no longer grabbed. Too bad that perch was cut almost through, so that we all tumbled down almost simultaneously: me, the pieces of two-by-six, and then a couple of seconds later, that small sheet of clear plastic fluttering down and landing nearby.

3.

The rest is kind of foggy for a while. There was no great pain or discomfort initially; nor was I out cold. I remember, for example, that the rain started, and that I knew I needed to get out of it and that I couldn't. I don't know how long I lay there; maybe fifteen or twenty minutes. Until he came back. Until he came back and as he approached me, I heard little whispered exclamations: "Oh, oh, oh," escape him as though involuntarily, until he was staring down at me with that face, so that the thought made me giddy: that man had a mother? And then paraphrasing: when he was born, did the midwife slap her? And he said, *Jefecito*, you must get up. You must not lie on the froze ground in the frozing rain, and as he somehow not only gets me up but onto his back, I keep saying, never mind, never mind; never more, never more, Lenore, Lenore. All this he informed me afterwards, so I consider it completely inadmissible. We sat there in his car, which he had left running, while he decided whether to bring me home or to the hospital, and as my head cleared somewhat, he decided on home, and I said, but the ladder, the ladder, but he didn't pay any attention to that. He just started driving and chatting; the chatting to help keep me from dropping off, though at first I swear I thought he was going to ask me for a raise.

He told me that the angel who whispered to him on occasion had told him to return to the job that night. No sooner had he gotten home and cleaned up than he knew he had to return. He had seen and heard the *Serpiente* out there directing the shingleros on our roof the day before, and then today the *Serpiente* was out there himself from a ladder with the *shizzall* for a few minutes, just a few minutes, making a cut. After. This was after he'd talked with me on the phone in the afternoon. He knew it was me the *Serpiente* was talking to on his new little biscuit of a phone that he was always using now as he walked around pretending to be Big Man. Then he was quiet for the rest of the afternoon, very quiet, very strange, acting very strange. When the day had ended he, Catocho, had felt very strange; that something was very not right and later he had decided that he must return.

He drives slowly and keeps making sure I don't nod off. My *torrito rojo*, I say, do you know that in Tay-has, that down in Tay-has there are lawmen, *entiende*? They ride big white horses, white horses with black polka dots, horses named Toto, or Tonto, or Booboo—something; anyway these lawmen, see, they rescue trains from their robbers and rescue little old ladies from being driven off their land by the banditos and the outlaws and all the bad hombres out there in those badlands of Tay-has, see? And sometimes they don't even bring in those band-aidos, those burr-itos, they just say, here, outlaw, in-law, take this piece and draw, and then bang-bang, no more outlaw in-law, see? Don't even bother to bring him in fer stringin up. Don't wanna waste the money of the good law-abidin cit-sinry on such extrapolaneous matters as jury trials, *entiende*? Cuz some folks jes need killin, jes bad seed, jes plum did not work out in acceptable fashion. Did he understand? But he's just going, uh-huh, uh-huh, uh-huh, like he does when it's all rolling right past him, and he doesn't have a clue what you're saying, which, I decided, wasn't such a bad thing under the circumstances, given that I didn't have a clue what I was saying either.

We drove in and Ellen took one look at me, listened to me babble for half a minute, then came to a different conclusion from Catocho's and raced me over to the hospital on the other side of Sterling. I sang a few of the old favorites on the way: *Good Night Irene, You Are My Sunshine, Candy Man*. I think she had about three suits on her tail by the time she pulled into the emergency room access drive, but she shut those boys up pretty quick with that look of hers and a few of the same choice expletives I'm sure she'd rather I leave out of the official record. So there we were checking out the old coconut again. By that time I was almost clear-headed and starting to hurt pretty bad everywhere I'd landed, including my neck, which after a few minutes is what concerns them most. The emergency room doc, who happens to be the same one who treated me the year before when I got clocked by the two-by-eight says, "What are you trying to do here, guy? We only have so much gray matter." And I say, don't I know it, doc? Before long I'll be able to read the same children's book over and over and not remember a thing about it and think it's just the latest and greatest every time. Or have the same idiotic thought over and over and think it's unique and brilliant and a great revelation each time. And he says, go home, and come back next week and don't do much of anything in the meantime and call me if *blah-di-blah-di-blah*, and seriously if this happens much more— Seriously, doc, it won't happen again if I have anything to say about it.

So we got home and I rested and Catocho finished the job without me, and they tore down the tower of terror without me, and I got thinking things over with all that time for the first time in such a long time, staring at the fire and watching my little girl play. Let's get out of here, I said to Ellen. Let's go up to the sticks. I'll build you whatever you want. I'm not so far gone that I can't build whatever kind of house you want: whatever size, whatever style, whatever materials. I can see she's looking at me like maybe I'm not all better after all, like maybe I've grown an extra head, and she just has a few vague comments about our daughter and her mom, knowing I'm not one hundred percent yet and need more rest. I'll get over it.

Which I suppose I did. I guess in some way I did just get over it. The cold snap broke; the ground thawed. I was up puttering around, feeling great for a man twice my age. Catocho was pretty sick of working at Junior's job site, I could tell. Not that he skipped any days. In some way they'd developed a way of working together, but Catocho was easy to work with, easy to be around. I didn't have to be there. He came to the cottages for a couple of days, and we worked on some light carpentry repairs. Mostly he worked, and I watched him work, made cuts and told him what to do. More and more this was getting to be the gist of our working relationship. I wondered how long before that was all there was to it. He was pretty sick of the *Serpiente's* job site; what could he do next? When could we start again with Mr. Pete? I'd check. Not yet, I thought. Not yet for me, I was sure. What about the foundation repair job just a few miles from Junior's project? Had Junior talked to him about it? No, he knew nothing about it. We'd go over there then. That would keep him busy for a few days, probably. After that I'd figure out a week's worth of projects here at the cottages. That wouldn't be hard to do. By then we could probably start in for St. Pete, his next project over on the mainland; start doing demo.

I went and looked at the foundation job, first with Junior, and then with Catocho. The foundation had two places where a little water was coming through: down from the side of a basement window halfway along a straight section of the back wall—you could see the crack where it started above ground at the side of the window—and then an inside corner, also along that back wall, where a deck extended from an interior living and dining area. A nasty spot to get at there under the deck, and we'd end up replacing some deck boards. Was he game? I needn't have asked.

Junior was glad I was feeling better. I was just at that age when things started to happen, he said. He had come down hard on the shingle boys for the way they'd left things on that roof. He had to have them go ahead with that roof while I'd been away, but it was totally unacceptable the way they'd left it. He wouldn't be using them again, but he'd have more work for me and the little guy, the little mook. His work was acceptable; he could keep filling in until I was ready to come back. I, I, Junior. Right away. Oh, and had he mentioned that I wasn't to tell anyone that he'd taken on this foundation job? Yes, indeed, I knew all about it. No one would ever know that he'd deigned to take this job on. I'd take it over, including the billing.

What a gloomy place this time of year. Fog settling in every day early in the afternoon. A dozen houses in that little development and not a soul around. Nothing but dense oak and pine woods, the trees all twisted and gnarled and nibbled bare of foliage up to about five feet. A nice enough house. Hard to figure, though, what people saw in such places, such locations, why they paid a fortune for an ordinary house in the woods. Three miles from downtown Sterling; that was the answer.

Catocho knew the drill. I'd drive out to check on him a couple of times a day; pitch in a little if I could. Junior would be by as well every day. The ground would be soaked, waterlogged, prone to cave-ins. We didn't need any more mishaps. As soon as he got the new tar back on the wall, he was to fill it all back in. Then we'd do the deck boards together. Fill it in immediately. *"Inmediatamente?"* he asks, looking at me, as I recall it now, clear as a bell. Yes. Fill it back in immediately. These jobs were nothing but a nuisance and a hazard. Catocho was the only one who liked them. The place made me nervous. Not a soul lived out there. Hundreds of houses and nobody home. Thousands of acres of woods. A couple of old rumrunner landings, which were now just boat launches, places for people to walk their dogs.

The location was convenient for both of them. Catocho and Junior. Two miles or so from Catocho's place; roughly the same distance from Junior's job site, though in different directions. I knew Junior would go out there and check on him, both because, despite what he'd said, he cared about the outcome. A perfectionist, was Junior, and you had to give him that much. In his way he was a perfectionist. And because he loved driving around holding a coffee cup acting like a big shot. For me it was closer to a fifteen-mile drive, but because the place gave me the creeps—I wanted to make sure Catocho didn't bury himself back there—and because I was feeling better, up and around, and it felt good to get out and do something, I drove over and checked on him twice a day, once late each morning and once later in the afternoon. I left him a screwgun, a stepladder, all the tools he'd be needing.

Sure enough, by the time I got there, going on noon the first day, he was almost done with the first excavation, the one along the straight wall, then had switched over and started pulling deck boards to get at the inside corner under the deck. Working under there would be a nuisance, but at least the ground would be drier. I helped him finish the first excavation, grabbing the full buckets as he passed them up, then went down in there to check the wall and the footing. It was so tight, I had to pass the ladder out and leave it up on the lip of the excavation in order to bend over and check the bottom of the wall. He was down far enough, about to the base of the footing. I couldn't tell how well the wall would clean up; he'd find that out tomorrow. You could see the little fissure where the water was seeping through the wall. The earth banks were waterlogged. All around water was oozing out of the ground and dripping, though it wasn't collecting under foot in a big way, just a thin, muddy layer over the firm soil. Perfect gypsy grave, I remember thinking, having read somewhere some tidbit about gypsy burials. The whole bank on one side was close to caving, which came to mind as I was using the hammer to scrape the base of the wall where it met the footing. One good push of the shovel with one foot, that's all it would take; the excavation would be half filled back in. Of course, this had to come to mind while I was completely stooped over, crammed in down there. Then he was standing up there looking down at me with that, at-your-service, attentive look. I had the same rogue thought as I'd had while looking up at him after falling off the roof. I guess I started to smile. Is okay? Yes, it's fine.

He passed me down the ladder, and I climbed out. I'd go get him the waterproofing mortar and the tar. Didn't we have enough tar for this job somewhere? We stargazed for a minute. Mr. Pete's, Catocho said, beating me as usual. He meant the last site over on the mainland. Too far. I'd buy a new can. By later that day when I got back with the supplies, he had the deck boards off and was finishing the excavation in the corner. Amazing. The man was a machine. Again we worked together to finish it. Barely enough room in there under the joists for all the excavated soil, but at least the ground was drier. All backfill. Easy digging, particularly for me since I hadn't done any of it. We couldn't see any cracks in there, but it didn't take much. He might see something when he had the wall cleaned up. By the time I visited him late the next morning, I was pretty sure he'd be applying the waterproofing mortar. Sure enough—like clockwork. No fooling around. No breaks. He knew the drill. I didn't have to tell him anything. If I chatted a little about what he needed to do, it was just to hear myself talk. For whatever reason, I repeated that as soon as he was done tarring the next morning, he was to start backfilling. You could see a fissure opening up in his pile of excavated soil there beside the excavation. The whole bank on that side was creeping in. Yes, he'd seen it too. He understood. He'd start backfilling. Tomorrow I'd bring the cedar deck boards to replace the slightly rotten ones, and we'd do that part together later in the afternoon. I wouldn't be back until then. That was fine. He was fine. I went over to the old landing not half a mile away to eat my lunch before driving home.

When I got back there with the deck boards the next afternoon, Junior's pickup was in the driveway. Just what I'd been looking forward to: a sermon from Himself. His driver's door was open; maybe he was in there working on something under the dash. No, he wasn't in there. There was a note, though, obviously intended for me, penned in that neat, almost feminine hand. "Mooky," it said—what a comedian, that Junior—*Mooky*—"left the base of the wall at the inside corner untarred and was starting to backfill. It is completely unacceptable." I've left out the huge letters and all the exclamation points that accompanied that last sentence. It was set off by itself. Took up most of the bottom half of the sheet. I could picture him back there lecturing Catocho on how it was done. 'Mooky' would never have left the base of the wall untarred. He must have done it on purpose. Must've done it for the sheer joy of watching Junior have a fit. I smiled at the thought. My little red bull; getting to be a prankster himself in his old age. So Junior himself was back there setting things straight. This would be good. I was looking forward to it. I wondered if his face would turn purple.

As I rounded the corner to the backyard, I heard the hum of a screwgun—mine, not Junior's. So they were replacing deck boards already. Must have smoothed things over, so to speak. Must be working together like two peas in a pod. Two amigos. The first excavation was already filled in and tamped down. Nice, neat tar line a couple of inches above grade. I felt that twinge, akin to jealousy, that I hadn't been the one to sign off, to inspect, but then, I'd told him myself to fill it back in when he was through. I imagined he'd waited until Junior had seen it. The filling in was a matter of a few minutes. The way those banks were ready to go—

Up on the deck, just Catocho screwing down decking. No Junior. Once he sees it's me, he sets down the screwgun. Stands up. Shaking. I looked below the joists—all filled in and tamped down. The neat tar line. The tamped earth. A little swollen looking, this one. A little bit pregnant. So odd the way he stands there, looking away, shaking like a leaf. I looked away again. Noticed the stepladder down on the lawn, leaning against the deck rail. No tar bucket. No brush. Then I looked back at the now former excavation, so neatly tamped down, then at him again, as he stands there, not saying anything, shaking. It took less than a minute for all this to transpire while something, while everything sinks in. I think I got out, "Where's?—" before it stuck, caught in my throat. As soon as I started to speak, it was as though a tremendous weight fell upon me, like an enormous wave or landslide. I reeled away and was only caught by the deck rail towards the backyard. He was shaking so hard I could feel it in the floor, feel it in the wood as he just kept standing there, waiting.

4.

He was in the dock. I would be pronouncing sentence. I would be the judge. No other sentence, no other judgment would matter to him. What I said and did would be final. I just stared out at the woods beyond the yard and the covered swimming pool. This was far too much. Dear friend. Dear little fool. You have buried us all. I stared out, not seeing, beyond thinking, in shock, as he just stood there, shaking. The whole deck was shaking. Out in the woods, among the oak trees are two deer, two young bucks at the edge of my view before the thickening fog closes in, bucks who, as I watch somehow become two young boys, Tom and Huck, young boys out in the ranchlands beneath the towering peaks of the Missions, who ride their bikes on the ranch roads and fish the irrigation ditches and the streams: it is Eden to those boys, that land, that life. One or the other of their dads is always bringing them out to the Flathead to fish from a skiff or the river to fish from its banks when the salmon are running, and then on their own as they grow, they go up into the mountains with nothing but their slingshots and their .22s. They know that in the mountains there are big cats still and some say a few grizzlies, at least on occasion, so they lie awake at night for hours, listening to every forest sound, every leaf, every twig. They talk for hours, contemplating such matters as, does the magpie really know everything? And how could the wise man possibly know that the magpie knows everything? Until the sky starts to promise the dawn. Then with their two friends from the rez— Thurlow (his first name) and Wolf Guts (his surname)—they devise elaborate games and wars and explorations, latter-day Lewises and Clarks, Crazy Horses and Red Clouds. There are organized games and sports, too, when it can't be avoided, in which everyone wants Thurlow on their side, who's better than everyone at everything, including math and chess. Then Thurlow goes off to a special program so that he won't get into the rez life, and Wolf Guts gets into the rez life in a big way, and it's just the two young bucks again who are growing antlers, are growing horns, so they need money for cars, money to treat teenage girls to whatever teenage boys imagine teenage girls wanting, so they work at anything that pays on the ranches and in town, clerking and stocking shelves, and haying and mowing and fixing. Fixing and repairing—there are manuals that teach you how to fix, how to build, how to repair. Through many tiny disasters that seem at the time like the end of everything and many finger-wagging lectures; with each job learning. Then they have a plan: they'll be partners; go halves. One will study architecture, the other engineering, and they'll see what comes of it; meanwhile working together through summers and vacations and then full time. He, the architect, graduates, while I—but how much engineering do you need to build houses? Who, when it comes to homebuilding, seem to mostly do their figuring and then say, double it to be on the safe side. How much engineering do you need to do that? So after a couple of years I start in with a mason and then a framing crew, and for a while, a concrete crew, and then he joins me. We will build, he and I, for he knows timber framing and conventional framing and is no more afraid than I, so we go off to the boom town, the booming cow town, to build our small, beautiful masterpieces, thought through in every detail and carried through with love and the joy of youth. We will build small, beautiful homes for loving young couples, for young families who will nurture happy, boisterous children in their well-sited, well-built small and then not-so-small, but still beautiful, still well-crafted homes. He is gaining something of a reputation, is the Baass, for his homes and has landed a first-rate little better half, and then their own little ones come right along. Then sometimes booms go bust, but what did we know of boom and bust? It was all boom. We were Supermen. Even when the young couples we build for lose their work and then stop paying, leave us hanging, leave us out with all our accounts, we'll come through it, won't we? We'll work our way through it as always, won't we? I land us a job, a house jacking: dig it out, new foundation, new sills, new everything in the basement, then renovate the house. It won't pay as much. It won't be like the masterpieces, but it's a job. It'll see us through. We'll work like kids, until the boom comes back. We'll work our way through it, like we always did. He grows quiet a lot of the time now. No more laughing. One day he just says quietly, too quietly, my name, so that I just wait. He repeats my name, quietly, then says, "I have a family. I have children." I just wait. Let him finish. He has a family. And he has a new plan. He will go back to school on the west coast, a school filled with natural light on a campus graced with enormous evergreens, and then he'll work in a firm on the west coast; they've made their offer. It's what he has to do for his family. Did I understand? Of course, I understand. Now turn in thy shovel and get thee out of mine basement. As if this weren't golden opportunity enough for any man. Go on. Beat it. No, he'll help me finish. No, he will not, now *gehen sie vamoosin* the hell out. So we laugh again, finally, like before, and I spend three more months underneath that house until my hands burn for the first, but not the last, time.

Do I blame him? Of course, I don't blame him. He would have been wrong; would have been remiss not to take his best shot for his family. As I would be, who have a family. Dear little friend. Dear little fool. I have a family. Can you understand? I must save my family, or at least try, as if that were possible after this, as if that were even remotely possible after this. So you must hang. I must let you hang. I must hang you.

I turned back to him, standing there still. Shaking. Awaiting his verdict. Awaiting his sentence. The only one that will matter to him. The only one that counts. "Pull the screws," was all I said. Yes, I was hanging him. I might as well have shot him. I saw his shoulders droop, and his head. His whole being slumped, became that of a man without hope. Then he bent and started in pulling the screws, carrying out his own sentence.

Only mid-afternoon. A thick fog was settling in already. I left him there to his work and went back around to the front. Junior's pickup with the door open. The keys there in the ignition. His hysterical note on the first sheet of the pad along the length of seat beside the driver's seat. *It is completely unacceptable*, with all those childish exclamation points. Hit the nail on the head this time, Junior. An understatement. Late Friday. He was headed off the island for the weekend. Who knew toward what rendezvous? Who wanted to know? Nobody. I closed the door. About a dozen houses in this subdivision and not a soul out here. Quiet as the grave. No delivery men, no postmen, no kids getting off school buses. Nobody. Still as death. And his repeated admonition: don't even tell anyone he'd taken this job on. He'd only taken it on for my benefit. And now such rank ingratitude. Wouldn't his face turn purple to think of it? I think I was verging on delirium by this point. Should I drive off to find a cop? I went back around first. Catocho had some of the deck boards back off already. I looked down under the joists again at the neatly tamped earth, the straight line of tar along the foundation wall up to the corner and past the corner for a few feet. That'll never leak. Good work. A job well done. The fog was dense now. I couldn't even see the woods I'd stared at before. I thought of the deserted neighborhood; his keys still in the ignition; that hysterical note. I just stood there mulling the whole thing over while he kept pulling screws. Then I noticed the screws: sheetrock screws. Not even deck screws. Where had he gotten them?

As I say, I've never read a convincing description of how this part happens, you know, the point when the lights come on, when all the pieces that have been swirling around come together to become something whole. Not that I'm claiming any particular brilliance about the outcome. I didn't make some great discovery. I wasn't curing cancer. In fact, if anything, the outcome points out something I've said any number of times: the creative process is value neutral. You can have an awful goal and achieve it brilliantly, and who's better off for that? Better to have a worthwhile goal and fail to achieve it. And these days, just deciding what's worthwhile and what's not can keep people tied in knots forever. I'll admit I had a bunch of pretty lousy options at this point. That's the other point: you have an idea that seems as though it'll work, but we can only see down the road so far. What seems a truly good idea at the time may be only an expedient solution that causes even greater problems down the road. And we can't possibly know that at the time of the decision. The light that comes on may be a will o' the wisp. Still I'll grant, at the time, at least, I sensed the outcome was somehow—acceptable.

My little red bull, did you somehow foresee all this? Or did you just get lucky? Did you know your quarry that well? And your *jefecito*? "Finish pulling those screws," I said, "you know we don't use sheetrock screws on a deck." But why get yourself so bent out of shape over an honest little mistake like that? Then get the cedar boards out of my truck and the saw and square and square head deck screws from my toolbox. Sheetrock screws on a deck! Imagine. "Let's go! We'll lose the light." For a moment he seemed frozen into place, kneeling there, until I admonished him again, this time telling him he was getting lazy in his old age. At that he seemed to come back to life; he fairly flew off the deck to do as I'd instructed.

It came together fast. There were really only a few pieces of decking that needed to be replaced. I angled the cuts from bottom to top and mated them together so that no gaps would occur with shrinkage. The rest was just cleanup. He had everything packed neatly into my truck as the light was failing. "Now go," I said. He was looking at me questioningly, looking at Junior's truck, as though to say, we no done yet, but I just said, "Go!" in a tone that wasn't to be questioned or doubted, though I nodded in answer to his look.

Junior kept his truck in good running order. I let it idle while I picked up the legal pad with the note on top. The first part was for me. I made a neat fold and tore the sheet across, put the top half of the note in my pocket and left the part about how completely unacceptable everything is on top of the legal pad, clipped into the clipboard. That part was for the world; for posterity. The landing, as I think I've already mentioned, was about a half mile away; certainly less than a mile, off another little side road. Nobody en route. Nobody parked there at the landing. No dog walkers. I didn't linger. Someone would be along. What a ghost town this time of year. It occurred to me again how a private security business would make sense for this side of the island. So many vulnerable houses; so few residents.

I parked along the side, out of the way of the boat launch area and the turn around, left the note on top of the clipboard right where it lay, put the keys under the mat—wouldn't want Junior's truck getting stolen—and closed the door. Then I noticed that little disk of a phone of his, beside the clipboard. I didn't like the looks of it somehow. I took it and closed the door again, then brought it down to the water's edge. Five skips. I knew those things were good for something. As I walked past the truck, I decided it looked as he might have left it. It wouldn't draw attention to itself. I didn't even bother walking back through the woods. The ticks are hungry when they're waking up. If anybody passed me, I'd just wave. Everybody's in their own little world out here; their own private movie. They probably wouldn't even notice me; might not even see me. I didn't even hurry, but there were no cars that night.

I checked around the house one more time and then drove home. I drove there once again in daylight that weekend. Everything neat as a pin. Not too long ago I drove back, just before beginning to write this. One-year anniversary. The deck had been repainted. The ground underneath didn't look pregnant anymore. I left flowers.

Chapter Eight

"All That We Are Is a Result of What We Have Thought."

CATOCHO WAS DEPORTED a couple of months later. I'd warned him not to let his wife drive. She didn't even have a fake driver's license. She'd get a ticket for, say, a stop sign violation and then more driving, and then another ticket for, say, speeding, and then more driving—all the time without a license. That may not be why their house was raided. Catocho's conditional status had expired, his request for asylum denied. That may not be why his house was raided either. Who knows? He spent a week in some kind of detention facility on the mainland and another month in an open-air facility in Arizona and then was shipped home. He calls from time to time from Catocholand. Has a cell phone. Everybody down there is getting cell phones now, apparently. I'll have to break down and get one soon. He's driving a lorry out in the hinterland, ferrying passengers and cargo using his own four-wheel drive SUV. Tells me Junior's been visiting his dreams regularly—down in his pit with his tar brush and his bucket, looking up pathetically, saying my name, pleading. My name, not Catocho's. That's his dream, not mine. I'll leave the dreams to him anyway. Mine have always been rather insipid. I can barely remember any of them.

You can't do anything around here without being reminded of Junior. Left his imprint everywhere. Junior and old Harold both. All those layers of construction and repairs and torn-out repairs, like the transcript, the archeological record of an endless feud, an endless battle, written in the cipher of construction, there for the reading for one with an equal understanding of the subtleties of the language, to understand what happened if not always why. The old man's record, of all that was built, started and stopped and then started again—always started again and completed. Always completed eventually. Built sturdy and lasting if not according to anybody else's guidelines, not according to anybody else's rules. Then Junior's: more ambiguous—a smaller record and a record of smallness, of things started and left; of the work of others, interrupted, short-circuited and then left. That which he'd completed, done perfectly, up to snuff, up to code, but so much started and then stopped, not for lack of funds or materials; just stopped, abandoned. A builder leaves his autobiography in what he's built and how he's built it, longevity at least partial evidence of quality, but the absence of the former not necessarily evidence for the absence of the latter. Here, after all, new actors need their own stage sets, need to wipe away the old and start fresh.

I don't give a thought to what will happen to anything I've built. Too busy with other thoughts. Too busy imagining arguments; legal arguments. You see, Officer, Your Honor, Your Majesty, he was my right hand, see? And in the end, my left. And my back. And my legs. And he saw that his head, that is my head, or my neck, was threatened, you see? So if you'll just follow my logic, if you'll just stick with me here, it turns out he was acting in self-defense. See? Doesn't that make perfect sense? Imagining that Your Honor does not see; that what Your Honor sees is a clear case of premeditation with malice; with a willing accomplice if not a mastermind. No, one imagines, the ladies and gentlemen of the jury do not see; that if you squashed this whole stinking scrawl into a one-line headline, that it would not look good for the old mudslinger. It would not look promising. Things would not be looking up.

Nor were Junior's medical records, which kept arriving and arriving, despite all of Ellen's efforts, in the least mitigating. He was a very sick puppy towards the end, was Junior. His health was in freefall. He was sliding down a slippery roof with nothing to stop him, nothing to cushion the fall, cushion the blow. Full-blown liver failure and no candidate for a transplant. No excuse there, last I checked. Hard to imagine what his last two or three years would have looked like. Wouldn't have been pretty. Based on all the evidence, it wouldn't have been fun to experience or to deal with or to be around. Still no excuse.

And he, my little red bull, is down there in

Catocholand, a right arm without a body; a body without a head, dare I say, without a heart? Not that he's running around like a chicken with its head cut off. He's back to living in the old way, within the old patterns. Exile is insufficient penalty, I suppose. How he misses his country. How he loved his country. What a man to have in the trenches. He gladly did our dirty work. Did I say our? Forgive me. Mine. My dirty work. It's all my fault. All of it. Mine, mine, mine. I, I, I. Dear God, that fool still cracks me up.

Ellen talks of another child. Her last chance, she says. Last chance. I look at her, studying her. Not for too long, I hope. Certain words, phrases do it for me. Lots of them, actually. Dear heart, I say eventually, you're no longer in your extremely late thirties. There are risks. "What is life without risks?" she asks. I don't know. You've got me there. Excellent question. She wants to try. For a boy. And what would we name him, I wonder? Let me guess. Welcome to happily ever after.

Junior's death, deemed a suicide, was likewise deemed totally unacceptable. Other than the death notice, not a peep in the paper. Only the most perfunctory of investigations. Searches of the harbor, only for form's sake. Strictly a formality. For anyone who understands the water out here, the fact that a body never washed up came as no surprise. Life is cheap out there in the bay. The fish-heads would've been far more surprised had a body turned up. What with all the shark sightings in the inlets. What with all the seals around now. More prey, more predators. It's only a matter of time before a surfer or scuba diver— Junior just joined the food chain. Chum, at last, and they laugh their cigarette-lung laughs. It kind of fits, knowing the man; kind of a fitting end, they say.

I take his part, defend him. I do. I picture him here on the grounds of the cottages, carrying the old man up the stairs to the second floor deck of Number 1. There's a great view of the harbor from up there. Carrying the old boy up there so he can look out over the grounds, the harbor pond, to the inlet and the jetty so that he can see his creation and all of the broader creation hereabouts on a warm summer day. Brings him up the stairs to enjoy a summer afternoon outdoors, Junior struggling under the burden while the senile old fool flails and curses, pummeling him with his fists and scratching at his face and cursing poor Junior, poor Harold Junior with a stream of invective, while Harold Junior says, over and over, "Oh, Pop; it's okay, Pop. Look at the view we're getting today, Pop," the old man calming down finally as Junior places him gently into the deck chair and lovingly bundles him up. They pick out boats they both know. Talk about the boats, their make, their captains; the catch recently. That's the image that keeps coming back to me. That's the one that won't leave me alone.

I added a stone to the memorial garden. The whole thing looks better to me now somehow. Junior's stone says, "Devoted son. Master craftsman." To his little niece, who's reached that *ask-Daddy-one-question-after-another* stage, I say, "Your uncle was a master of all trades." From the day she's learned to speak, it seems, she speaks in complete sentences, soaks up whole piles of words at a time. Tries to imitate her mom in everything.

Already swims well; loves clamming, playing in the mud. There is a mood that sometimes strikes this flaxen-haired angel, when her face grows dark and gloomy and she scowls, and my blood positively freezes. If she spoke with his voice at such times, it couldn't startle me any more. They're flesh and blood. No getting away from him here, or anywhere out here. Or anywhere else.

Happily ever after. And what would we name our little boy, I wonder? I leave her, leave them, who sleep so soundly, to walk around the grounds at all hours. No crawling around under the cottages. No nocturnal missions. Only daytime repairs for me, after announcing my presence. My mudslinging days are over. My hands and arms are getting better. My knees are shot. I have a busted gut. Residual arthritis. From Lyme disease. No, not yet. No spastic colon yet. All self-inflicted. We choose our own paths. We have free will. What? Think I'm trolling for sympathy? How I'd laugh. How I'd laugh in your face.

Anyway, this little interlude is all done. Time's up. Soon the men will be here for me: José, B, and C. *É* will be doing some spring cleanup here on the grounds. B and C will start on some light work on one of the properties we manage. One of the Golden Geese. I took over some of his accounts. We keep it light: yard work, some repairs and maintenance, some staining and painting. They show me their papers; I don't ask them any questions. *Trabajo, dinero, cerveza.* One breaks, I go down to the convenience store and get another. At the end of last year I handed the whole mess of paperwork over to the accountant. Let him figure it out. We have lots of bills to pay. The old place has piles of debt. When you look around the grounds and then the broader neighborhood, you have to wonder about the logic of a place like this. If we just broke off a building lot or two—Ellen likes the place just the way it is. Ellen and the old lady both. She takes her mom out for leisurely strolls around the grounds and over to the memorial, the little one romping around nearby them. A vision of Eden. Three sweet little peas in a pod.

Now to build this its home: one last job on the mainland. I've been putting it off. How quaint: a hand-written scroll, rolled up and sealed inside a tube, then buried in the backing wall of some masonry. Lots of buried work in masonry. It can't be helped. It's the nature of the—beast. It's sure to turn up some day. Until then, the stones are mute. The earth is mute.

www.ingramcontent.com/pod-product-compliance
Lightning Source LLC
Chambersburg PA
CBHW070845120626
46556CB00002B/890